Praise for
It's About Time

This is a very interesting mystery novel. The idea is fresh and the storyline is compelling. It was truly an interesting read. Miller has written a fine and suspenseful mystery novel. It truly merits publication.

—B. E. Baldwin
Librarian and Judge for Draft to Dream Competition

Get ready for a laugh-filled caper in Courtney Miller's *It's About Time,* an excellent new entry in the field of geezer-lit mysteries. Ex-homeless man, Frank Roberts, teams with four other geezers to form the Sleuthkateers to solve the case of a poisoning death in a retirement home.

—Mike Befeler
Author of *The Tesla Legacy* and
the *Paul Jacobson Geezer-lit Mystery Series*

COURTNEY MILLER

It's About Time

It's About Time, A White Feather Mystery by Courtney Miller

Books may be purchased in quantity and/or special sales by contacting the author or publisher at:

www.PopulvuhPublishing.com

Popul Vuh
Publishing

Cover Design: Nick Zelinger, NZ Graphics
Interior Design: Ronnie Moore, WESType Publishing Services
Editing: John Maling, Editing by John, and Margaret Ireland
Book Consultant: Judith Briles, The Book Shepherd

Published by: Popul Vuh Publishing
PO Box 91
Westcliffe, CO 81252

ISBN: 978-0-9887711-7-8(Hardback)
ISBN: 978-0-9887711-8-5(Paperback)
ISBN: 978-0-9887711-9-2(e-Pub)

Library of Congress Control Number: 2017941383

1. Native American—Fiction   2. Cherokee—Fiction
3. White Feather (Fictitious Character)—Fiction   4. Murder Investigation—Fiction   5. Wet Mountain Valley—Fiction

First Edition   Printed in USA

Acknowledgments

I am so thankful for all of the great friends, authors, and professionals who helped with this book.

The idea for "geezer lit," that is, writing about old geezers, for old geezers, by an old geezer was inspired by the trend-setting author, Mike Befeler.

I owe a great debt of gratitude to Sheriff Shannon Byerly of the Custer County Sheriff's Office for helping me understand the procedures and dynamics of a real, rural mountain valley sheriff's office.

Once again, the great publishing team has put together a beautiful book. The team was led by Dr. Judith Briles, The Book Shepherd. The editing was done by John Maling, Editing by John, and Margaret Ireland. The cover was designed by Nick Zelinger, NZ Graphics. The interior layouts were done by Ronnie Moore, WESType Publishing Services.

And a special thanks to my wife, Lin, whose support, help, and advice is invaluable.

This book is dedicated
to all the old geezers out there.

Other Books
by Award-winning Author
Courtney Miller

The First Raven Mocker
Book 1 of The Cherokee Chronicles
> Has received a Beverly Hills Book Award,
> International Book Award, and NIEA Excellence
> Award for Historical Fiction

The Raven Mocker's Legacy
Book 2 of The Cherokee Chronicles
> Has received a Book Excellence Award for
> "Literary Excellence in Faction" [Fiction based
> on Fact]

Gihli, The Chief Named Dog
Book 3 of The Cherokee Chronicles (coming soon)
> Finalist in the 2015 Extravaganza Draft to
> Dream Book Competition

Ludwig's Fugue
Book 1 of The White Feather Mystery

It's About Time
Book 2 of The White Feather Mystery
> Winner of the 2016 Extravaganza Draft to
> Dream Book Competition

St. Jude

Chapter One
Let Us Pray ...

*O most holy apostle, Saint Jude, faithful servant and
friend of Jesus, the Church honoureth and invoketh thee
universally, as the patron of hopeless cases, and of things
almost despaired of. Pray for me, who am so miserable.
Make use, I implore thee, of that particular privilege
accorded to thee, to bring visible and speedy help where help
was almost despaired of. Come to mine assistance in this
great need, that I may receive the consolation and succor of
Heaven in all my necessities, tribulations, and sufferings,
particularly (my last days) and that I may praise God with
thee and all the elect throughout eternity. I promise thee,
O blessed Jude, to be ever mindful of this great favour, to
always honour thee as my special and powerful patron, and
to gratefully encourage devotion to thee. Amen*
—Catholic prayer

Judy muttered a prayer as she opened the envelope.
The return address was for St. Jude Methodist Retirement
Home. She pulled out the letter and scanned it quickly.
She let the tear run down her cheek. Her prayer had been
answered.

Sunday

Chapter Two
7:00 A.M. Rescued

Franklin Damon Roberts sat at one of the many long tables at the Canon City Homeless Shelter and cupped his steaming bowl of oatmeal with his tattered wool gloves hoping to thaw his frozen hands. His body was still chilled "to the bone" after a long, restless night in his cardboard box under the bridge. But tonight would be different. His name was on the list for a bed in the shelter.

"Good morning, Frank." Her bright, optimistic voice shocked him out of his numbing funk. It was coming from a world he was no longer a part of. He was part of a world where survival was the only tenant. Judy lived in the civilized world he had left behind five years before.

Frank looked up slowly and blinked to focus on the pretty face of the happy, thirty-ish woman whose innocence and sincerity drew him out like an electric connection to his past, to a time when he was a part of her world. He managed a smile and a nod.

Judy reached over and touched his wrist. "You look like you're freezing."

"Bad night," Frank explained as he involuntarily shivered. "Tonight, I have a bed."

Judy smiled brightly. "Oh, you have more than a bed tonight, Frank!"

Frank frowned. He never knew what to expect from his favorite shelter volunteer. She had always treated him with a bright smile and an encouraging word. He braced for one of her optimistic phrases. She had always treated him as an equal, not some hopeless, homeless person to be pitied. In reality, she had not treated him markedly different from others, but had always made him feel like her special friend.

Her exuberant voice framed in an air of sophistication, breeding, and education drew him out of his trance. "I have wonderful news to share with you." She patted his wrist and looked deep into his eyes.

"There is an opening at St. Jude Methodist Retirement Home and they have accepted your application."

Frank looked at her bewildered. "I don't remember applying."

Judy sat back as if embarrassed. "Well, I took the liberty."

Frank looked down at his oatmeal. He was starving, but somehow felt it would be rude to eat in front of her. "What is it?"

Judy shifted to the edge of her chair, placed her hands on the table and sat very straight with an ebullient smile on her face. "It is a very nice place, Frank. It was once a tri-county hospital and is a charming old brick building on a lovely one-hundred-acre estate. There are lots of trees and a lake and grassy lawns. It is quite exclusive and difficult to get accepted."

Judy glanced down at the aging oatmeal. "Oh, please eat your breakfast before it gets cold."

Frank was stunned by her overwhelming news. From her description, he pictured the place in the movie *Rainman*. He looked down at the oatmeal that had formed a crust and had ceased to emit steam. He took the old spoon and stirred thoughtfully, but he had lost his appetite.

Frank felt grimy, filthy, and smelly sitting in Judy's elegant new Mercedes. They had driven through that part of Canon City he had made his territory since losing everything in the great recession. As they passed the park where only the derelicts were welcome, he gazed upon the destitute, one of which he had become and been obliged to befriend. He had never felt a part of that crowd, and now he found himself quickly reframing his view of them, his old "territory," and himself.

Sitting beside Judy in her elegant vehicle, his self-esteem slowly began to return and he began to feel "normal" again. He had been a successful executive in several major corporations and private businesses. He was well-educated in his own right and could have driven a Mercedes once had he preferred it to his Jeep Grand Cherokee. Now he owned nothing but the clothes he was wearing.

They were soon out of the old commercial district and winding through modest, well-kept craftsman houses and bungalows before easing into the quiet downtown area. Frank stared silently out the window, captivated by the journey that was a metaphor for the internal transition going on within him.

They drove by the old prison on Highway 50 and made a sharp turn to skirt the slice of limestone rising up on the west side of the city like a giant knife blade and were soon climbing up the winding highway as the town and his homeless life were indeed fading away behind them.

Judy tried to start a conversation, and they settled the matter of the weather and each remembered an experience on the terrifying one-way road aptly named "Skyline Drive" that crowned the limestone knife blade.

After climbing over rolling hills where the Royal Gorge tourist town and famous suspension bridge lay quietly sleeping, Judy gave an update on the great fire that had temporarily shut it down and the status of reconstruction.

Highway 50 descended into a beautiful, deep canyon carved out by the Arkansas River. The raw, wild, rocky canyon seemed a far cry from the dirty park and deteriorating commercial district where he had spent the last five years of his life.

They saw fly fishermen casting into the wide river as they drove further and further along the winding canyon road. The serene canyon had captured Frank's thoughts and, for the last fifteen minutes, he and Judy had just sat quietly in the car watching the road twisting and turning beside the river.

Judy leaned forward and squinted as she slowed to make a turn onto Highway 69 that climbed out of the canyon into a long valley separating the massive peaks of the Sangre de Cristo mountains on the west side and the rolling peaks of the Wet Mountains lining the east side. As the valley widened, there were patches of forest mixed with meadows where cattle grazed on sprawling ranches. Small herds of deer grazed along the road and seemed confused by the passing car.

They drove on and on until the forest thickened and Judy pointed to a lush, green hill to the front, right. "There it is, Frank."

He eagerly searched for "it" as the car slowed and Judy turned on the right turn signal. Ahead, a plain green sign unceremoniously announced "St. Jude Methodist Retirement Center."

As Judy eased into the turning lane, Frank resumed his search. In the distance, a small forest was split by a wide, asphalt road leading up a large, rounded hill. An impressive old brick building with a conical center tower crowned the top of the hill. *That must be it,* he thought.

The large facility disappeared behind the trees as they entered the thick forest and climbed the long hill. Suddenly, a large clearing opened up and St. Jude Methodist Retirement Center loomed at the far end. The face of the building was broken up by two identical protrusions on either side with the hexagonal, conical tower in the center. Frank counted four stories with the tower rising another story above the rest.

To some it might look massive and imposing, but to Frank it looked warm and appealing, like a beautiful castle full of hope and promise. Judy offered her opinion, "It's such a charming old building. It is over one hundred years old."

Chapter Three
8:00 A.M. Home Sweet Home

A SMALL PARKING LOT was carved out of the lush yard in front of the left section of the grand building at St. Jude Methodist Retirement Center. There were only a few cars parked in a neat huddle in the corner closest to one of the two entrances. As Judy stepped out of the car, she pushed a button on the key fob and the trunk lid clicked. She retrieved a bulging athletic bag and handed it to Frank.

"What is this?" he asked as he took the bag.

Judy smiled, raised her eyebrows and tilted her head to one side. "Oh, just some clothes and things. Hope they fit."

Frank looked at the incredibly thoughtful woman. "Thanks."

As their shoes crunched loudly on the gravel in the parking lot and they drew closer, the age of the ancient building became readily more apparent. Frank noted that the small, covered porch entrance was quite unimpressive compared to the grandeur of the rest of the building.

Inside, they had entered an average size room decorated like a cozy living room. An elderly, neatly dressed black woman sat behind a small desk in the back corner of the room. The woman looked up and smiled when she recognized Judy. "Well, good morning Miss Judy."

"Good morning, Naomi." She turned to Frank. "This is Frank Roberts."

Naomi smiled at Frank. "Welcome to St. Jude, Mr. Roberts."

Frank smiled awkwardly. "Thank you. A pleasure to meet you." He had grown unaccustomed to meeting people formally and strained to recall her name.

Naomi nodded and looked at Judy as she picked up the phone. "I'll call Mrs. Barkley to let her know you've arrived. She's expecting you."

Judy nodded and then led Frank to one of the inviting couches near the center of the room. "It's quaint, but comfortable, don't you think, Frank?"

Images of his cardboard box under the bridge flashed into his head, "Oh, yes, quite nice."

Judy smiled at him. "I think you will find it a most pleasant place to live. The staff is very friendly and helpful. There are a lot of fun activities. I think they really care about the residents here."

Frank's mind was hung up on the irony. Judy's life was so far removed from his that she could not possibly see this building through his eyes. To him it was a warm shelter, maybe a comfortable bed, three meals a day. It meant not having to live in a cardboard box anymore. Anything more was just "gravy." In fact, this room was "too nice" to be comfortable for him.

Naomi interrupted, "Mrs. Barkley is on her way down. How about some coffee or tea or something?"

Judy turned to Frank, "What would you like, Frank? I'm sure you must be thirsty after the drive."

Frank glanced around the room. He was not accustomed to having a choice. Tap water at the park was his staple, but in a fancy place like this he felt compelled to request something special. "Iced water maybe?"

Judy nodded and added, "Tea for me. Two sugars, please."

Frank shifted on the couch. He felt so dirty and was ashamed of his worn clothes. He decided to leave on his coat even though the room was quite warm, for fear his smelly body odor might escape. "Where is everyone?"

Judy glanced around and then explained, "Oh, this is just the reception area. The residents have a grand living room inside and several recreation rooms. I expect they seldom come out here."

Frank raised his eyebrows. "What a shame; seems like a waste."

Judy nodded and glanced around the modest room. "Yes, I suppose."

Frank read into her response an indifference born of a more lavish lifestyle. He guessed that she might have rooms in her house that received only occasional use. Five years in poverty had trained his mind on efficiency.

Naomi returned with their drinks and Frank eagerly enjoyed the cold, delicious water. "Want a refill?" Naomi inquired smiling warmly.

Frank was embarrassed. He had gulped down the water boorishly. A door opened and a slender, young woman burst in beaming a grand smile, "Judy! So good to see you again."

Judy popped up, set her tea on an end table, and smiled. "Hello, Edith. Good to see you, too."

Edith Barkley charged across the room and grabbed Judy's hand and then offered her hand to Frank as Judy introduced him, "This is Frank Roberts. Frank this is Mrs. Barkley, the Administrator for St. Jude."

Frank jumped up, accidentally shoving his glass into her hand, jarring ice cubes out on the floor. Humiliated, he shifted the glass to his left hand and tried again. Mrs. Barkley had a firm grip and shook his hand enthusiastically. "It is such a pleasure to meet you, Mr. Roberts. Judy has told us so much about you."

Frank glanced at Judy sheepishly wondering what she might have told them. "It is a pleasure to meet you." He could not say that Judy had told him anything about St. Jude.

Naomi had picked the ice cubes up off the floor and discretely retrieved the glass from him. Mrs. Barkley clasped her hands and suggested, "How about a tour?"

Judy added, "Oh, yes, I can't wait for Frank to see this place. It is such an amazing old building and you have done so much with it."

Frank nodded. "That would be great."

She smiled and turned toward Judy. "Oh, thank you, we try. You can leave your bag, Mr. Roberts. We'll be back down here after the tour."

She led them through a large double door into the intersection of two long, wide corridors. Mrs. Barkley led them to the end of the east-west corridor and pointed out the staff dining room and lounge on the left. She stopped at tall, double doors and explained, "This goes out to the back lawn."

They back-tracked to turn down the north-south corridor where she stopped to point out the entrance to the large dining room on the left filled with six-place oval tables. On the right side of the corridor was a parlor and library. Another reception was in the northeast corner and the medical facilities down the other east-west corridor.

They returned to the center of the floor to the elevators. There were two sets of elevators, one with silver doors, the other with bright red doors. Barkley explained that the red doors were off limits to the residents since that elevator ran to the top floor where the administrative offices were located. They took the resident elevator, with the silver doors, to the second floor where the administrator pointed out the large Craft and Activities room, which Frank imagined was probably directly above the ground floor dining room. Next to it was a larger game room with card tables, TVs, and pool tables. The back wall was lined by tall windows looking out over the back lawn and lake and provided a spectacular view of the Sangre de Cristo Mountains. Across the corridor from the Craft room was a parlor with comfortable chairs and couches for reading or quiet reflection and a nice view of the front lawn and the Wet Mountains in the distance.

Mrs. Barkley explained that resident rooms lined the perimeter of the floor. "Ready to see your room?"

The third floor was dominated by one large corridor running north-south with narrow hallways branching off the west side. A parlor with comfortable chairs, several card tables and a view of the front lawn was on the east side and centered on the corridor across from the elevators. Frank's room was the first room on the right past the parlor further down the corridor. It was a small interior room with no windows. A regular sized bed was just to the right as you entered the room. To the left an old recliner sat in the corner and, to the right of it, the door to the bathroom. A chest of drawers was centered on the back wall.

The bathroom was shared and had a large window looking out over the east lawn. To the left, a small lavatory was tucked into the corner next to the window, and to the right, a large shower accessible by wheelchair dominated the south wall. After all the spacious public rooms they had viewed, Frank was disappointed with this "cubby hole," but he took a deep breath and forced a smile. "Home sweet home."

Mrs. Barkley turned to Judy, took a deep breath and declared, "Well, let's get you signed in."

Judy did not budge. She was studying Frank. "What do you think, Frank?"

Frank felt bad. He sensed that she had detected his disappointment. He did not want her to think that he did not appreciate what she had done for him, "It is truly an amazing place, Judy. I am pretty overwhelmed right now."

Judy perked up. "So, do you think you can live here?"

Frank's heart lurched and he felt giddy and a little scared. "Definitely."

Mrs. Barkley clapped her hands. "OK then." She pointed her hand toward the door. "Let's do it!"

Chapter Four

11:00 A.M. Settling In

JUDY HELPED FRANK UNPACK, explaining each item in the bag and where it had come from. She seemed to enjoy organizing his chest of drawers and helping him get settled. Frank enjoyed her company and wished he was half his age. Thankfully, she did not seem to notice his attraction for her.

As she placed the last item in the bottom drawer, she pushed it shut, tossed her hair back and stood. "Well, that's it. Can you think of anything else you might need?"

Frank had watched her from the comfort of the soft recliner. He sighed. "No, Judy, you have thought of everything. I can't tell you how much I appreciate what you are doing for me."

Judy beamed. "I am just so happy for you, Frank. You deserve a break."

She glanced around the room and scowled. "How dreary. You need something on the walls!"

A young girl peeked in the door. "Mr. Roberts?"

Frank leaned to one side to get a better look. "Yes? Come in."

The girl entered and stared at Judy who reached out her hand. "I'm Judy, Mr. Robert's friend and sponsor. I was just helping him get unpacked."

The girl grabbed Judy's hand and shook it vigorously. "Oh, hi! I'm TJ. I just stopped by to meet our new resident and to escort him to the dining room if he's hungry." She turned to Frank and raised her voice. "Are ya hungry, Mr. Roberts?"

Judy looked at him and smirked. Frank's stomach growled softly as if responding for him. Frank shrugged. Judy nodded. "Well, OK, I should be going. My husband is probably getting hungry, too. I'll stop by Thursday to check on you, Frank. In the meantime, if you need anything, you can call me."

She took a card out of her purse and laid it on the nightstand by his bed. Frank pushed himself out of his chair. "Thanks again, Judy."

She brushed his arm, smiled and stopped by TJ. "The room could use a picture or something. Do you have anything?"

TJ twisted her mouth and looked up. "I don't know. I'll see."

As Judy strolled out, TJ smiled at Frank and asked, "Ready?"

Frank suddenly felt filthy again. "Can you come back, TJ? I haven't had a chance to take a shower yet. I sure would like to clean up before lunch."

"Oh, sure!" she replied. "Need any toiletries?"

Frank waved her off. "Oh, no, Judy has me all set up. Thanks."

"OK, then, I'll be back." The bubbly teenager rushed out.

Frank started to close the door but an old lady with stringy white hair stood in the way. "Who are you?" she demanded.

Frank flinched. "Oh! I'm the new guy, Frank. Who are you?"

She eyed him very carefully before answering, "I'm Lizzie ... your neighbor." She poked her thumb over her shoulder and glared at him.

Frank tried to smile. "Nice to meet you, Lizzie."

He glanced behind him. "I don't mean to be rude, but I was just about to ..." When he looked back, she had vanished. He leaned out to look down the corridor expecting to see her shuffling toward the elevator, but the corridor was empty. He looked in the direction she had indicated with her thumb, but the corridor was empty in that direction as well. He shook his head, shrugged and closed the door. He paused for a moment and then locked the door. He did not want another "neighbor" wandering into his room while he was in the shower.

He had always heard the expression "peel your clothes off" but had never truly appreciated the phrase before. He had not had a shower in so long that his clothes were literally rotting on his body. He piled them in the plastic trash can so as not to contaminate anything else in the room.

The bathroom and shower were quite large, almost half as large as his room. He noticed the door connecting the shared bathroom to his neighbor's room. *I share a bathroom with Lizzie?* he thought. Fortunately, he could lock that door from the inside.

The hot, steaming water felt wonderful as he lathered and rinsed and lathered and rinsed over and over hoping to scrub off the grunge that had built up after years of being homeless.

As he dried off, he stared out the large window at the lush, green lawn, the thick surrounding forest, and the rolling mountains in the distance. He grabbed his toiletries and stood before the sink and aging mirror. His pale shoulders and chest looked fresh and clean, but his shaggy face and wild hair still looked like that of a vagabond. He brushed, or more like scrubbed his teeth and as he swished and was ready to spit, there was a knock on the door. He spit, rinsed quickly, wrapped his towel around his waist and rushed barefoot to the door.

It was TJ. She gave him a quick look over. "Too soon? I can come back. Oh! I found a calendar for your wall."

She handed him the 8.5" by 11" spiral bound calendar. He nodded shyly. She spun around and hurried back down the corridor. Frank closed the door, pitched the calendar on his bed and returned to the lavatory. He tried to pull a comb through his hair. The comb glided through *like a rake through alfalfa,* he thought. It had been a long time since a comb had slid through his hair without snagging.

He rubbed his chin and considered not shaving, but then decided he wanted to see himself clean shaven. When he patted off the leftover shaving cream, he was almost shocked by his appearance. The octogenarian admired his youthful face and declared, "I look like a seventy year old!"

He laughed at his private joke, gathered up his toiletries and returned to his bedroom. He opened the chest of drawers and was almost overwhelmed. He proudly donned fresh underwear, fresh socks, fresh pants, fresh shirt! What a wonderful feeling to be human again. Judy had even provided him with new canvas sneakers.

He walked over, opened the door and left it ajar. He was ready; he was eager; he was excited to make a grand appearance in the dining room. *Lizzie will not recognize me,* he thought. Suddenly, a tall, hunching old man shuffled in and headed straight for the bathroom. "Hello?" Frank challenged.

The old man stopped, turned and grumbled, "No need to lock the bathroom door unless you want me coming through your room every time!"

Frank flinched. "Oh, I'm sorry. I forgot!"

Frank held out his hand. "Frank Roberts."

The tall, stooped old man with a large nose, wrinkled face and thinning white hair ignored his hand. "Ralph."

Frank smiled and added, "Pleased to meet you, Ralph."

Ralph continued toward the bathroom. "Fine. Now if you'll excuse me."

Frank chuckled as the grumpy old man disappeared into the bathroom and slammed the door.

Frank took a deep breath and tried to sit in the recliner to wait for TJ, but he was too restless. He decided to hang the calendar on a nail already in the wall next to the chest of drawers. He flipped over the pages to the correct month and hung it up.

He stepped back to admire it and then returned to the recliner. His thoughts were interrupted by Ralph gargling loudly in the bathroom. He sat for a few moments and then jumped up and removed the calendar. He checked the back and sure enough, it was blank. Judy had used a marker to label his clothes and left it on the chest of drawers. He took it and drew a large circle on the back of the calendar. Counter-clockwise he wrote the abbrevia-tions for the months ending with DEC at the top of the circle. On the spot where the current day would be, he placed a hash mark, smiled and hung it back on the wall. He had never liked square calendars. His diagram reflected the way he pictured the year in his head.

He tried pacing in the room for a while. The toilet flushed and through the closed door, he could hear Ralph's clothes rustling and the rasping cough of the old man trying to clear his throat. Frank decided to venture down the corridor to watch for TJ.

Chapter Five

11:45 A.M. Benjamin Cook

Frank had toured the third floor again and paced the corridor to the point his legs were getting tired before TJ finally arrived. The effervescent teenager flew out of the elevator and crashed into him, "Oh! I'm sorry."

Frank held her arms. "It's OK, I was just pacing."

"Mr. Roberts? You look so different. You're ready?" she gushed as she spun out of his grasp and offered him her crooked arm. "Well, let's go."

The dining room was a sprawling room filled with eight large, oval tables hosting six per table. The tables were covered with white tablecloths, the walls hosted prints of the masters in traditional wide, wood frames, and the dark, oak walls hinted of a grand, by-gone era. Floor-to-ceiling windows lined the back wall offering a stunning view of the back lawn, small lake, and magnificent mountains. The clatter of dishes and rumble of voices was disturbing for a man who had lived for years alone in a cardboard box under a bridge. Even during rush hour, the bridge was not as chaotic or noisy.

"Where would you like to sit?" TJ asked.

Frank searched the grand room. "Do you have a window seat?"

"Ooh," she said through her puckered lips. "Let's go see."

It was obvious that a window seat was in high demand, but there was one table by the windows where a single, rotund, black man sat by himself. TJ seemed to ignore it so Frank offered, "How about over there with the big guy?"

TJ's nose crinkled as she glanced around the room. "Well, maybe you'd prefer somewhere else."

Frank was a little put off by what he assumed was her racial bias. "No, that table's fine."

She squinted. "Are you sure? Benny is ..."

"I'm sure." Frank insisted.

Reluctantly, she led him to the table. As they approached, Benny smirked. "TJ! Come 'ere little girl and give ole Benny a big hug."

TJ grimaced and tried to introduce Frank. "Mr. Cook, I'd like to introduce our newest resident, Mr. Roberts. He wants to join you."

Benny reached out and grabbed TJ around the hips and pulled her up to him. "Of course! Nice to meet you, Roberts."

TJ struggled to free herself as the forward man handed her his big, empty tea glass. "Would you be so kind as to bring me some more tea, perty thang?"

She elbowed her way loose and wagged her finger at him. "Don't you ever do that again!"

Benny grabbed his chest and stuck out his lower lip as if she had hurt his feelings. TJ stormed off with the glass in a huff. Benny motioned to the chair next to him. "Sit down, Roberts, tell me about yourself."

Frank pulled back the chair and sat down tentatively. "Not much to tell. Been homeless since the great recession. Been livin' in a box under a bridge, just gettin' by."

Benny laughed grandly. "A man with no false ego. How refreshing!"

Benny raised his hand, waved and shouted, "Woody! Over here!"

Frank turned to see a short, skinny man with a large hook nose and wild, curly hair surrounding his kippah, carrying a tray of food. Despite his comical appearance, he seemed quite reserved and distinguished. He took a deep breath, nodded to acknowledge Benny and reluctantly dragged himself over to the table. "This is the new guy, Roberts. Roberts meet Woody."

Woody set down his tray across the table from Benny, sat down, clasped his hands and placed them on the edge of the table. "Contrary to my jovial friend's belief, I am not Woody Allen. My name is Albert Stein."

Frank smiled and reached across the oval-shaped table to shake his hand. "I am Frank Roberts."

TJ bounded up and slammed the refilled glass of tea in front of Benny and then dashed off before he could grab her, touching Frank's shoulder as she flew by. As Benny watched her departure, he dumped about three tablespoons of sugar into the tea. He declared in a deep, melodious voice, "Now there goes a truly vivacious young girl. My, my."

He laughed uproariously at himself as he stirred his tea and turned to Frank. "Wouldn't you say, Frank?"

Frank glanced at her and nodded. "Oh, yes, she has plenty of energy."

Benny added, "She makes me tired just watchin' her," and then laughed again.

He turned to Albert. "How about you, Woody, what do you think of my little TJ?"

Albert took a drink of water and shrugged. "She is out of your league, Benjamin."

Benny laughed. "Woody don't talk much, but when he does ..."

Albert glanced up at Frank and winked, then picked up his fork to begin eating. Noticing that Frank did not have a tray, he stopped and glanced around, motioned to a lady wearing a white apron over a blue dress, held his hand over Frank's head and pointed. The lady nodded and headed for the cart full of trays parked by the kitchen doors in the back of the room.

Albert explained the procedure. "When you come in, you can grab a tray off the cart. There is another cart with glasses of tea and water over there." He pointed.

Frank took a deep breath. He thanked Albert and tried to make conversation. "How long you two been here?"

Benny scooped up a fork full of noodles. "I've served ninety-six days of my sentence so far." He stuffed the fork into his mouth and looked at Albert.

Albert shrugged. "Almost a year."

Benny chuckled as he took a bite of bread and gulped down half of the sweet tea.

The lady with the apron placed a tray in front of Frank and asked, "What would you like to drink, sir?"

Frank thought a moment and then ventured to ask, "Do you have milk?"

The kind lady smiled. "Of course."

Benny declared, "A milk man!" then laughed heartily.

Frank shrugged. "Just craved milk for some reason. Haven't had any in so long."

Frank soon learned that Benjamin liked to keep the conversation rolling even if it meant doing all the talking himself. Frank took a lesson from Albert and tended to the business of eating and tried to ignore the obnoxious, boisterous man.

Chapter Six

Tweedle Dee and Tweedle Dumb-Dumb

Benny spotted someone. "There's Twiddle Dee and Twiddle Dumb-Dumb."

Frank glanced at the entry to see a large, distinguished looking man dressed formally in a brown suit and tie with a tall, stout, smartly dressed woman clinging to his arm. As they shuffled along, the woman appeared to be prompting him surreptitiously.

Benny turned to Albert. "What's their names, Woody?"

Albert lowered his fork and turned to look. "That is Mr. and Mrs. Benaford Wilson, Benjamin."

Benny shook his head. "Mr. and Mrs. Looney Ben." He laughed loudly and downed the last of his tea.

Albert whispered to Frank, "Mr. Wilson has dementia. Mrs. Wilson is the keeper of his memories."

Benny leaned back. "Is that what she does?" The rotund man closed his eyes and wheezed. Frank watched the couple and could not help but admire the way Mrs. Wilson helped her husband maintain his dignity. He could tell that she was a remarkable woman.

Benny scoffed loudly, "He looks so dignified. It's comical."

The couple glanced toward Benny prompting him to laugh at them. Albert kept his head down and continued eating. Frank felt very ashamed of his boisterous colleague, but Benny just mocked the proud man. "Hey, Wilson!"

The reserved man stared at Benny as his wife whispered something in his ear. Benny commanded, "Come over here, Wilson!"

Albert scolded through his teeth, "Benjamin!"

The confused man glanced at his wife. She whispered to him again. He glared at Benny. Benny persisted. "Don't be rude, Wilson. Come over here!"

The man appeared embarrassed and intimidated. He glanced at his wife, then looked around the room before shuffling over to Benny's table despite his wife's contempt. Benny motioned to two empty chairs. "Sit down, Wilson. You too, Mrs. Wilson. We have a nice view here, don't you think?"

Wilson obediently sat down. Mrs. Wilson politely whispered to her husband, "Stay here, darling. I'll go get our trays."

Benny lifted his empty tea glass. "Since you're going that way, Mrs. Wilson, would you be so kind as to fetch me some more tea?"

Mrs. Wilson glared at the arrogant man, exhaled in a huff, grabbed the glass and marched off. Benny grinned slyly at Mr. Wilson. "She's right handy, ain't she?"

Wilson turned to search for her. "Oh, yes, she is a wonderful woman."

Benny's attention turned to the next person entering the dining room. "There he is ... our token Injun!"

Frank and Albert turned to see an old man with wild, straight white hair pulled through a round deer bone at the top of his head. A white feather dangled to one side. Benny found the stooped and weathered old man comical. "Good 'ole White Feather." Benny patted his mouth with his hand and shouted his imitation of a war whoop.

The Native American sporting a long, colorful shawl draped over his shoulders stopped and glared at Benny before proceeding toward the cart full of trays in the back of the room. Albert commented, "Maybe he will scalp you."

Mr. Wilson giggled giddily. Benny laughed loudly and then raised his hand to wave grandly at a hefty black woman entering the room from the kitchen. "Hi, Birdie!" he yelled.

Birdie stopped and glared at Benny with a condescending look. She shook her head in disgust as she wiped her hands on a towel. Benny was delighted. "Now that's a fine woman. A FINE woman. Lordy!"

Albert muttered, "Maybe she poisoned your noodles."

Benny feigned surprise. "Whoa, Woody, that woman loves me."

Albert shook his head. Frank watched the friendly chef stop at each table and visit. He could see that she had the ability to light up the faces of the people sitting at the table. She made them smile and laugh and they clearly loved her.

Mrs. Wilson returned with two trays and set them down on the table. Benny raised his eyebrows. "Forget my tea?"

The tall, sturdy woman glared at him and walked off. In between bites, Albert commented, "You couldn't see that her hands were full, Benjamin?"

Benny scowled at his friend. "Well, excuuuuse me, but I'm thirsty."

Frank glanced back at the tea tray and saw Mrs. Wilson dumping a spoonful of white powder into one of the tea glasses. The old Native American stepped up beside her and set down a tea glass as he adjusted his grip on the food tray in his other hand. Frank noticed that Mrs. Wilson slid the Indian's glass over beside her glasses inadvertently. White Feather picked up another glass nonchalantly and Frank watched him find a table far from them near the back wall. Frank was privately thankful that Benny did not see the "token Injun" dodging him. Benny was too busy complaining about the bland food while at the same time shoveling it in as if he found it delicious.

Someone caught his attention across the room and with a twinkle in his eye, he fluttered his fingers at her. Frank looked across the room and spotted a sixty-ish, attractive black woman fluttering her eyelashes at Benny. And in turn, Frank caught Benny fluttering his eyelashes back at her, grinning stupidly.

"Girlfriend?" Frank asked.

Without taking his eyes off the flirting woman, he declared, "My sweet Katie Mae! MMM MMMM!"

Albert explained, "Benjamin imagines that he and Katherine are an item."

Benny frowned and retorted, "We ARE an item! In fact, Miss Katie Mae is coming over to my place right after lunch."

Benny grinned grandly and then winked at Frank suggestively.

Mrs. Wilson returned with three large glasses of tea squeezed in her fingers forming a triangle. She set them on the edge of the table next to her tray and then with all eyes trained on her, placed one in front of Mr. Wilson's tray and one in front of her tray. Then, as if forgetting the other glass, sat down ignoring Benny.

Benny gasped and held out his hands crying, "What about me?" Frank and Albert laughed as Frank handed the glass to the apparently bewildered man.

Chapter Seven

Murder Most Foul

Benny TURNED HIS ATTENTION to Frank and began a relentless oratory on the history of St. Jude. Frank remembered that Judy had told him that it was once the county hospital and had been purchased by the Methodist church when the hospital closed. The church had remodeled it and converted it into a retirement home for the indigent.

Benny's version was much more sinister and mysterious. "Originally, this was a looney bin—a state institution for the insane."

He paused to laugh. "It was built in 1891 and don't ask me why, but it was modeled after that creepy Hudson River Institute for the Insane in New York. This place became notorious for the maltreatment of its patients. There were some stories there, Woody!"

Benny turned to Frank and whispered, "Woody was a newspaper reporter in his previous life."

Albert smirked and continued eating while Benny resumed his story. "When they finally closed the place, they found bodies hidden in the basement and patients running around naked, all drugged up and crazy as loons." Benny's eyes sparkled with delight at the thought.

He chortled as he glanced around the room. "It appears to have returned to its roots, hasn't it?"

His wandering eyes stopped on the stringy haired woman that had stopped by Frank's room earlier, Lizzie. She was glaring at Benny with wild, fiery eyes. Benny began to sing, "Lizzie Borden took an ax and gave her father forty whacks and when the job was nicely done, she gave her mother forty-one!"

Lizzie jumped up and rushed to their table wagging her finger at Benny. "Shut your mouth, you stupid man!"

Two of her friends jumped up and grabbed her arms. "Ignore him, Elizabeth, and come finish eating."

Elizabeth strained against their grasp. "Their ghosts still roam these halls, nigger. Mark my words, you don't want to mess with them."

Benny responded angrily, "I don't know if you're a ghost or alive, but your bigotry is alive and well, honky!"

Elizabeth's face turned to an eery calm. "One night they'll grab you around the neck and you won't know what's happening to you until they've strangled you to death!"

Birdie appeared. "Benny, what have you done now? Calm down, Elizabeth, pay no never-mind to this old blowhard."

Elizabeth glanced at Birdie, turned back to spit at Benny, then let her friends lead her back to their table.

Birdie reprimanded him, saying, "Benny, why can't you keep your mouth shut?"

Benny was angry and restless. He grabbed his tea and gulped down the last quarter of it, slammed it down and shivered. "Where'd you get this awful tea? Must've been left over from the asylum."

Birdie frowned, picked up the glass and smelled it. "What'sa matter with it?"

"It's bitter and tastes like it's a hunnerd years old."

Birdie replied, "How would you know with all that sugar in it?"

A loud noise drew their attention to Mr. Wilson. His tray was dumped in his lap, food covered his suit and he had a scared look on his face. Mrs. Wilson jumped up, grabbed a napkin, laid the tray flat on his lap and started swiping the food off his tie, shirt and suit lapel onto the tray.

Birdie threw up her hands. "Oh, dear. I'll get a wet cloth."

Mrs. Wilson stopped her. "No, that's alright, Birdie. We've finished. I'll take Benaford up to the room to change."

Benny guffawed while announcing to the room, "Benaford? Poor little Benaford spilled his tray." Benny glanced around and pointed at the flustered man.

Birdie shook her head. "Hush, Benny, you behave yourself or I won't get you any more tea."

Benny winked at her and slapped her behind as she left. She turned, wagged her finger and then cautiously backed away. Benny laughed grandly and then scooped up some noodles on his fork and resumed his story. "After the war, they turned this place into the county hospital. That lasted until around 1975 when they built that modern monstrosity in Canon City."

Without catching his breath, he scooped more noodles into his mouth and continued, "That hospital cost me my job, you know. It sits right where the hotel was where I used to work as the con-see-urge. It was a good job too. It was the finest hotel in town. But the owners got too old and sold out so they could tear it down and expand that dang new hospital."

Birdie returned with fresh tea. "Try that."

Benny poured a heaping serving of sugar into it, stirred it ceremoniously and then took a little sip, then a bigger sip, then gulped down almost half of the rest of it. He sat back, smacked his lips, swirled the tea in the glass and then downed the rest of it. He looked up at Birdie, raised his eyebrows and proclaimed, "Worst batch yet!"

Birdie punched her fists into her broad hips and scowled at him. All of sudden he dropped the glass, vomited all over his chest, grabbed his neck and began coughing. His face flushed and he started gasping and convulsing violently. Frank and Albert were stunned. Birdie started slapping him on the back. "Somebody call the nurse!"

Benny flailed about in his chair as if something invisible had a hold of his throat and was throwing him around. Lizzie came running up shouting, "I told you! I told you they'd get you!"

In one final lurch, the bedeviled man slammed forward and buried his face in his tray leaving everyone stunned. Katie Mae dashed across the room yelling, "Benny! Benny!"

She elbowed past Lizzie and threw her arms around the collapsed man, wailing and shouting his name over and over. Nurse Nujent rushed in, pushed her aside and pulled his head back. "Call 9-1-1!"

She swiped his mouth with her fingers. "Help me get him on the floor."

Albert, Frank and several men from another table pulled the hefty man off his chair and laid him out on the floor. "Give me room!" the nurse shouted. As everyone backed away, she began resuscitation.

Standing over her, the sixty-ish, attractive black woman screamed, "Benny! No!"

Lizzie threw back her head and gave out a horrifying, maniacal laugh, "I warned him!"

Chapter Eight

1:00 P.M. 9-1-1 Call

Undersheriff Buster Crab was alone in the Wet Mountain County Sheriff's Office when the call came through. The dispatcher, Deedie, rang him on his phone. "Chief, there's been an incident out at St. Jude's. A man is dead and the ambulance is on its way."

"I'm on it. Notify the sheriff."

Buster grabbed his hat and jacket and rushed out of the office. His uncle-in-law, Benny Cook, came to mind. He had managed to get his uncle accepted at St. Jude after his wife, Buster's aunt Ellie, died. Benny had not settled in well and he had been called out to talk to him several times. Benny had not been liked by the family, but his aunt Ellie had stood by him. As he stepped out of his office, he turned and shouted, "They say who it was?"

Deedie responded, "No, sir."

He rushed out and jumped into his SUV. As he stopped at Seventh Street, coincidently, the screaming ambulance raced by. He turned on his siren and followed it through town and out Highway 69 north. As he raced past the ambulance, he radioed Deputy Morrison. "Sam, you get the call?"

The staticky radio answered, "Yes, sir. I'm getting on 69 at Copper Gulch Road."

Buster could see the flashing lights on Morrison's SUV sitting at the intersection ahead of him. "Roger. You want to escort the EMTs, I'm going on ahead."

Chapter Nine
1:05 P.M. Aftermath

THE RESIDENTS OF ST. Jude were still in shock when Mrs. Barkley, the administrator for St. Jude, charged into the dining room and took over. She first ordered all residents to remain in the dining room until further notice. She explained that she suspected the sheriff would want to question everyone.

Suddenly, the receptionist, Naomi came running in screaming and crying. Albert whispered to Frank, "Naomi is related to Benjamin."

Mrs. Barkley grabbed Naomi and pulled her away from her uncle-in-law and the busy nurse trying to revive him. Naomi buried her head in Mrs. Barkley's shoulder and wept.

Frank and Albert moved away from Benny's table and found empty chairs at the old Indian's table. Albert politely requested, "Mind if we sit with you, White Feather?"

White Feather nodded and then pulled his brightly colored shawl tight around him. Frank and Albert sat down in chairs that gave them a view of the entire dining room. As they waited, Frank listened to the ghost stories shared among the residents at nearby tables. Frank whispered, "Think he'll make it?"

White Feather closed his eyes and shook his head as Albert proclaimed, "I fear our friend Benjamin has expired."

Frank reflected on the certainty of his friend's answer. He looked over to see that Nurse Nujent was still tirelessly working on the unresponsive body. He admitted to himself that he had also sensed there was no hope.

He had never witnessed anything as frightening as watching a man apparently being choked to death by some invisible entity. Images of the struggle flashed over and over in his head. Frank looked at his silent friends. "Do you believe in ghosts?"

Albert looked down and rubbed his hands. "I don't know. I've never seen one that I know of, but I have interviewed many who claim they have seen or heard them."

Frank was confused. "You don't think we saw a ghost just now?"

Albert inhaled deeply. "I don't know. I didn't see anything tangible even though it did appear we were witnessing the effects of something attacking Benjamin."

White Feather added in a quiet, soft voice, "The soul of the spirit will search for the ancestors, but may linger when confused. We should not call his name."

Frank shuddered and pondered White Feather's words. "Lizzie was convinced."

Albert huffed and nodded his head. He glanced around and then leaned close to Frank for privacy. "I don't know if Benjamin knew, but his little song probably hit too close to home. You see Elizabeth is a former resident of the State Institute for the Insane. She was committed when she was just a teenager to this very building and spent several years in treatment for weird behavior."

Frank gasped. "Oh, my gosh!"

Albert glanced around and then continued, "She was released to the family in 1945 when the facility was shut down. Shortly afterward, her mother and father died ... well, suspiciously. Their house burned down and arson was suspected. There were rumors that Elizabeth was behind it. The Police Chief in Pueblo confided to me, off the record, that he believed she set the fire, but he couldn't prove it."

"Why was she in the asylum?" Frank asked.

"I was never able to learn for sure, the records at the institute were transferred to Denver and sealed, but her aunt claimed that Elizabeth was possessed by the devil and her parents were afraid of her. Before she started acting weird, she had worked at the steel mill's clinic in Pueblo as a nurse's aid. A neighbor told me that he thought she had access to drugs and got herself messed up. I suspect that was more likely what happened."

They could hear emergency vehicles pulling up to the entrance with sirens blaring. A large man in uniform rushed into the dining room and embraced Naomi. Albert explained, "Undersheriff Crab is related to Naomi and Benjamin. I think he was Benjamin's nephew-in-law."

A few minutes later, two EMTs and two more deputies rushed in. The EMTs quickly took over for Nurse Nujent. The poor woman stood back and then collapsed into a nearby chair. She was sweating and completely exhausted. Mrs. Barkley sat down next to her and patted her on the shoulder.

The EMTs worked on the body for several minutes before the sheriff rushed in and stood over them. "Sheriff Sean Bailey," Albert explained.

The EMTs looked up at the sheriff but did not have to speak. The sheriff nodded. Naomi and Katie Mae broke down again. Albert nudged Frank and nodded toward Katie Mae. "Benjamin's girlfriend."

Undersheriff Crab comforted his cousin and led her to a chair where the cook, Birdie, took over. Katie Mae was comforted by her friends at Lizzie's table. The sheriff, his deputies and Mrs. Barkley gathered around Buster, and seemed to be giving him moral support.

Frank grimaced. "Oh. That's sad."

Albert nodded. "Yeah. Buster Crab has done everything he could to get old Benjamin to calm down and try to fit in. But, Benjamin was an unhappy man. Maybe his soul will rest in peace."

White Feather startled them with a rebuke, "His soul won't rest if you keep calling his name."

Albert and Frank stared at the strange old Native American. Albert nodded. "We meant no disrespect, White Feather."

White Feather closed his eyes and nodded almost imperceptibly. Frank was at a loss for words. He looked back as the EMTs covered the body with a sheet. He could hear the sheriff shouting into his phone loudly ordering a crime scene investigation team. Then the sheriff huddled up with his deputies for a brief conversation before calling Mrs. Barkley back over. While they were conferring, Frank's eyes wandered over to Lizzie who was sitting silently with her friends. He thought he could read in her eyes and face a smug satisfaction.

Frank shook his head and turned to Albert. "What happened to Lizzie after the house burned?"

Albert shrugged. "She moved in with her aunt for a while, but was rebellious and eventually ran away. I found her in Denver years later and she had married. She seemed sad but pretty normal at that point, although reluctant to talk about her past, especially her time in the Institute. I didn't press her too hard. I already had enough for my article."

Frank stared out the window at the magnificent mountains looming in the distance. Albert continued, "Benjamin, oh! Excuse me, White Feather. Our friend was right about the stories. Clearly, the staff and administrators were in over their heads and a lot of atrocities occurred. Eugenics was big back then and I have no doubt that Elizabeth witnessed, and possibly experienced some pretty horrific things."

Frank frowned. "Eugenics? I thought that was a Nazi deal."

Albert took a deep breath and glanced at Frank before delivering what appeared to be a difficult explanation. "Yes, you are partly correct. But, in the first half of the twentieth century, eugenics or 'Social Darwinism' had a huge following in the United States and many other countries. In the U.S., many prominent scientists, doctors, and psychologists actively promoted the notion that we should promote improving the human species by discouraging reproduction by people with so-called genetic defects and encouraging reproduction among people with desirable traits."

Frank tried to soak in the implications of Albert's broad definition. "How did they discourage reproduction?"

Albert shook his head and held out his hands. "In many different ways, but in the mental institutions, there is good evidence that sterilization was practiced."

Frank gasped. "Oh, I see."

He could not help remembering the atrocities of the Nazis. "No gas chambers?"

Albert looked at him and then chuckled. "Oh, no. Nothing so extreme as that, but socially repugnant by today's sensitivities."

Frank remarked, "Man, it must be difficult for her to be back here now."

White Feather startled them with a question. "She have any children?"

Albert's eyes darted toward Lizzie. "No ... ," he said thoughtfully, "I don't think she ever did."

Chapter Ten

3:15 P.M. Possibly Strychnine

As THE CRIME SCENE investigators wrapped up their investigation of the body, the EMTs zipped up the body bag and started loading it on a gurney. The sheriff huddled with his deputies. "Well, looks like we've got a homicide."

Undersheriff Crab, Deputies Calhoun and Morrison traded glances. A tall, thin man with a long, chiseled face joined them. Sheriff Bailey continued, "Miles, I think you know everyone. Want to share what your preliminary investigation has turned up?"

Miles Blakeley, an agent with the Colorado Bureau of Investigation, nodded. The crime scene investigation had been handled by CBI out of Colorado Springs since the Wet Mountain County Sheriff's Office lacked the resources. Blakeley seemed impatient and condescending. "We think the victim was poisoned, probably strychnine."

Buster shook his head. "Benny finally pushed someone to the edge. We all joked about it, but apparently it was no joke to someone."

Sheriff Bailey added, "We won't know for sure until we get the autopsy report, of course, but let's proceed on that assumption for now."

Deputy Morrison, who had joined the Wet Mountain County Sheriff's Office recently after working as a homicide detective in Denver for many years, added his expertise. "When we interview these people, remember that they are all possible suspects. We are looking for motive and opportunity."

Deputy Calhoun popped off, "I can tell you that right now! They all had opportunity." Calhoun was right, but Morrison was irritated by how easily he jumped to that conclusion. The ex-homicide detective from Denver cautioned, "A good detective should keep an open mind and follow the facts."

Sheriff Bailey nodded and motioned for the administrator to join them. He introduced her, "This is Edith Barkley, St. Jude administrator. Edith, this is Sam Morrison and Jessie Calhoun. I think you know Buster Crab. And this is Agent Miles Blakeley with the Colorado Bureau of Investigation."

The attractive, professional looking woman smiled and shook their hands, then turned to Bailey for clarification. "Investigation?"

Bailey shifted. "Edith, we think Benny was poisoned. We will be conducting a homicide investigation. CBI will be heading it up and we will be working jointly with them."

Mrs. Barkley gasped. "Homicide? You think someone deliberately poisoned him?"

The sheriff nodded. "It would appear so, yes. We're going to want to question everyone."

Mrs. Barkley nodded. "Yes, of course, I held everyone back just in case you wanted to talk to them. So, everyone that was here when he died should still be in this room."

Deputy Morrison commented, "Excellent."

Miles Blakeley pulled up a chair for her and held out his arm, "Perhaps I could ask you a few questions to get things started?"

The confident woman appeared surprised. "Oh! Well, OK, how can I help you?"

As Blakeley pulled up a chair facing her, the sheriff and deputies remained standing. Blakeley arrogantly pulled out his glasses case and slowly, deliberately unfolded his reading glasses and placed them so that they clung to the tip of his nose. As he took out his notepad and pencil, he smugly looked over his glasses at her. "How long has Mr. Cook lived here?"

Edith crossed her legs and placed her interlaced fingers on her knee. "Well, I think it has been about three months." She looked up at Buster Crab. "That sound about right, Buster?"

Buster nodded, "Yeah, that sounds right."

Blakeley frowned at the large undersheriff, then back at Mrs. Barkley and continued, "What sort of a resident was he? Was he settling in OK? People like him?"

She glanced up at Buster again and then addressed the CBI agent candidly, "I'm afraid not very well. I'm sure it was very hard for Benjamin to accept his situation. He must have been sad and lonely since his wife passed away. I think he was acting out to cover his grief and desperation."

Blakeley raised his eyebrows. "Acting out?"

Mrs. Barkley shifted and pulled her hands back to her lap. "He was very loud and antagonistic. He irritated a lot people."

Blakeley got to the point. "Enough to push someone to want him dead?"

Mrs. Barkley made it clear. "To WANT him dead? Yes, I expect a lot of people would've liked to see him at least gone. The dining room had become his stage and he seemed to thoroughly enjoy humiliating the other residents and staff. Perhaps he thought he was being clever or humorous, but most people just resented his behavior."

Blakeley made some notes and then looked up from his notepad. "Were there any attempts to discipline Mr. Cook?"

Mrs. Barkley huffed. "Oh, yes! I know Buster has been out numerous times to talk to him, I've talked to him, Birdie has scolded him, well, just about every day."

Blakeley put down his notepad and glared at Under-sheriff Buster Crab. "Why were you called out, Crab?"

Buster glared back. "Mr. Cook was my uncle-in-law."

The tension between the two was palpable and appeared to be deep rooted.

Blakeley made more notes and asked while still writing, "Who is Birdie?"

She clarified, "LaWanda Beaudreau, Our cook. Birdie runs the kitchen." She pointed out the large, black woman comforting Naomi.

Blakeley studied her for a moment and then nodded. "How did he respond to your actions?"

Mrs. Barkley looked to Buster as if seeking help. "In different ways. He basically resented our efforts."

She chuckled. "One time after Buster visited with him, he locked himself in his room. After several days, we got worried about him and decided we were going to have to do an intervention." She looked at Buster and giggled. "So, Buster and Naomi went up to his room and when they got there, they heard giggling coming from inside. It turns out he had a lady friend sneaking food up to him."

Everyone but Blakeley laughed as Buster added, "We decided that for the sake of the other residents, we would just let him keep up his ruse. Unfortunately, today he decided he'd had enough of his room and returned to his old antics in the dining room."

Blakeley appeared to be ignoring her as he continued to write in his notepad. He glanced up looking over his glasses at Mrs. Barkley. "Was there any consideration given to removing him from St. Jude?"

Mrs. Barkley got serious and recrossed her legs. "Yes. In fact, he was on his final probation. Had this not happened, we would have been forced to discharge him."

Buster shook his head. "We should've done something sooner. I'm sorry, Edith."

Edith's eyes widened. "Oh, Buster, we all hoped he would come around. Sometimes they do. It's not your fault."

Blakeley seemed impatient. "Perhaps you could point out who I should talk to next?"

The gracious administrator surveyed the room. "Well, Albert Stein sat at his table usually. Elizabeth was one of his favorite targets. You should talk to Birdie about whom he attacked today. She was on the front line when it came to having to deal with him."

Blakeley looked around at the sheriff and deputies standing around him and hunched his shoulders. "Bailey, why don't you and your team go interview some residents."

He turned back to Mrs. Barkley. "Want to send over that Birdie woman?"

Mrs. Barkley showed her contempt. "You mean Mrs. Beaudreau?"

Blakeley appeared to be preoccupied with his notes and did not respond. Mrs. Barkley stood and stomped over toward Birdie.

Bailey smirked. "You heard the man, let's go interview some residents."

Undersheriff Buster Crab was clearly irritated and could not hold himself back. "Better watch your step, Smiles, or you'll wind up in one of Mrs. Beaudreau's famous soups."

Buster's colleagues including Sheriff Bailey collectively mouthed "Wow!" and reflexively stepped back. The nickname "Smiles" was a derogatory moniker here-to-fore only used behind the uppity agent's back. It was a clever formulation of his first initial "S" and his middle name "Miles" and referred to the fact that he almost never smiled.

Without missing a beat or even looking up, Smiles countered, "I'll take that under advisement, Tarzan."

"Oh-ho-ho!" his friends echoed. "Tarzan" was a reference to the actor Buster Crabbe who played Tarzan in movies in the twenties and thirties. The father of Undersheriff Buster Crab was a big fan of the Olympic swimmer turned actor and had called his son, whose birth name was William Gilbert, "Buster" from the time he was a baby.

"OK, OK ..." Sheriff Bailey held out his hands as if herding sheep away from a wolf and moved his deputies off to the side. "Let's put together a list and start our interviews. These poor people have been sitting in here for over two hours waiting for us."

Chapter Eleven

3:30 P.M. Birdie's Testimony

The NORMALLY JOVIAL HEAD cook for St. Jude, LaWanda "Birdie" Beaudreau, was nervous, almost scared as she took a seat in front of the stern, no-nonsense agent from CBI.

Birdie was an overweight black woman with a pretty, round face. Mrs. Barkley introduced her to Agent Blakeley and then excused herself. Blakeley looked up and nodded. "Mrs. Beaudreau, I understand you run the dining room?"

She raised her hands and shrugged. "Well, I am the head cook, yes, sir."

Blakeley continued, "For how long?"

She blotted her teary eyes with a crumpled tissue held in trembling fingers and nodded. "About five years now, Sir."

Blakeley appeared to glare at her. "I understand Mr. Cook was a handful."

Birdie reared back, shook her head and huffed. "Lordy! I guess so."

"Mrs. Barkley tells me that you had to scold him a few times?"

Birdie looked him in the eye and nodded sincerely, "Oh, yes, sir! Every day."

Blakeley probed, "What did he do that caused you to have to step in?"

She leaned forward. "Benny was a mean man. He was just a bully and loved to roil people, especially the weak. If he thought he could intimidate you, he would make you miserable. And he enjoyed doing it, too."

Blakeley made some notes and then readied his pencil. "Was there anyone he picked on more than others?"

She sat back and pursed her lips. Her temples were rippling as she studied him. Then she opened up. "He did have his favorites. I thought Miss Lizzie was going to scratch his eyes out a couple of times. Poor little TJ rushed out in tears today. Mrs. Wilson! Oh, Lordy, that woman has given him some looks! I swear her eyes could've burned a hole through him."

Blakeley wrote down the names and brief descriptions as Birdie had described them. "Do you remember who was sitting at Mr. Cook's table today?"

Birdie's eyes rolled up. "Lemme see now, there was Mr. Stein, of course." She looked at Blakeley. "He almost always sits with Benny." She briefly raised her hands as if balancing imaginary trays. "Don't ask me why. And the Wilsons were there for a short while. Oh! And there was the new resident."

She leaned over and put her crooked finger beside her nose. "What is his name? Frank, I think."

Blakeley finished his note and studied Birdie for a moment. She was just beginning to relax, but his next question changed that. "Mrs. Beaudreau, we ..."

"Call me Birdie, everbody does."

Blakeley kept a stern face. "We think Mr. Cook was poisoned."

She gasped and covered her mouth with her hand as Blakeley continued, "Where would a person get poison around here?"

Birdie frowned. "What kind of poison?"

Blakeley scowled at her. "Well, we won't know for sure until after the autopsy, but we suspect strychnine."

Birdie's eyes widened. "Strychnine?"

She rubbed her face with the palms of her hands as she thought about it. "I can't imagine where someone would get strychnine. Mrs. Nujent wouldn't have that in the pharmacy would she?"

Blakeley questioned, "Mrs. Nujent? Pharmacy?"

Birdie explained, "Nurse Nujent keeps the residents' drugs in the infirmary."

"Where is that?"

Birdie pointed back behind her toward the kitchen. "Oh, that's on this floor past the kitchen, down the hall-way on the north side."

Blakeley glanced around the dining room. "Is Nurse Nujent in here?"

Birdie raised her chin and scanned the room. "Hmm. Don't see her. She was worn out after trying to revive Benny. I bet she went somewhere to lie down."

Blakeley glanced at his notes. "Can you think of any-one else that might have wanted Mr. Cook dead?"

Birdie waved her hand at him. "Are you kidding? Everyone wanted that man bumped off."

Blakeley looked up at her with a smirk. "Could you be more specific?"

Birdie laughed loudly and slapped her thighs. She looked around the dining room. "OK, Mr. Stein had reason enough; Benny harassed that poor man all the time. Called him Woody." She laughed, put her hand beside her mouth and whispered, "He does look like Woody Allen."

Blakeley glanced around and spotted Mr. Stein easily based on her description and wrote his name down. Birdie continued, "Oh, and White Feather! Benny would pat his mouth and yell like an Indian when that poor old man would come in. White Feather ignored him. But I wouldn't mess with that man. He knows all that voodoo stuff."

Blakeley perked up. "Voodoo stuff?"

Birdie nodded. "You know. He's an Indian Shaman or witch doctor or whatever they call it.

The unimpressed agent looked around the room. "Where is he?"

Birdie glanced around and found him sitting at a table by the wall. "He's over there sitting next to Mr. Stein with the funny hair, colorful poncho, sleeping."

Blakeley found him and made a note. "Anyone else?"

Birdie pointed and flicked her finger as if checking off names on a list. "There's Lizzie. I told you about her." She held her hand next to her chin ready to point again. "I guess those are the main ones he picked on, but really, he picked on everyone and me and my staff and all the staff here."

She leaned forward and slapped his knee. "Deputy, you got your work cut out for you!"

Agent Blakeley almost came up out of his chair. "AGENT! I'm a CBI AGENT, not a deputy."

Birdie smiled warmly. "Same thang, ain't it?"

Blakeley huffed. "That'll be all, Mrs. Beaudreau."

Chapter Twelve

3:35 P.M. Albert Stein's Testimony

UNDERSHERIFF BUSTER CRAB SAT down with Albert Stein. "Good afternoon, Mr. Stein. Good to see you again. How've you been?"

The distinguished version of the actor Woody Allen shook his hand, smiled, and offered, "My condolences, Undersheriff Crab."

"Well, thank you. But please, just call me Buster."

Stein grinned. "Please, don't call me Woody."

The two men laughed. Buster knew that his uncle had picked on Mr. Stein by calling him "Woody." "Albert would be nice."

Buster nodded. "Certainly, Albert, I know Benny gave you a hard time and I hate that."

Albert shrugged. "It was hard for Benjamin. We all knew how he felt and hoped he would find a way to adjust."

Buster shook his head, opened his notepad and got down to business. "Birdie tells me that you were sitting at Mr. Cook's table today."

Stein nodded, but did not elaborate. Buster urged him on. "Can you tell me about what happened?"

Mr. Stein nodded and clasped his hands. "Well, it was vintage Benjamin Cook. He was in exceptional form today. When I arrived, the new resident, Mr. Franklin Roberts, was already at the table. Benjamin introduced us. Of course, he introduced me as 'Woody.' It was his pet name for me. I'm sure he thought that it irritated me."

Buster broke in, "Did it?"

Mr. Stein smiled. "Of course." He shrugged as if to say "What can you do?"

Then he continued, "TJ brought a glass of tea to Benny and I could see that he had already gone a round with her. She was very perturbed, slammed his tea down and stormed off on the verge of tears. A server brought Mr. Roberts a tray of food and he ordered milk to drink. Benjamin loved that! Then he began giving Mr. Roberts his version of the history of this august building until he spotted the Wilsons."

Buster interrupted him, "So TJ brought him his tea. Do you know if that was his first glass?"

Mr. Stein shrugged, but added, "I doubt it. He already had his food and had eaten part of it. So, I would guess he had imposed upon TJ to refill it. That was his M.O."

Buster was scribbling fast. "Hmm, OK." He was impressed with Mr. Stein's composure. His testimony was very practiced, well-organized. Normally, people were nervous and rambled during questioning. Stein seemed to know exactly what to report. It made him wonder if Stein had been involved in other investigations. "What did you do before retirement, Albert?"

Stein squinted at him. "I was an investigative reporter for *The Denver Post.*"

Crab raised his eyebrows and nodded. "You said that Benny spotted the Wilsons?"

"Mr. and Mrs. Wilson had just entered the dining room and were looking for a place to sit. Benjamin spotted them and hollered at Mr. Wilson inviting him to join us. Mr. Wilson has acute dementia and Benjamin likes to make fun of him. Mrs. Wilson is very protective of her husband and resents Benjamin's snipes."

Stein continued, "And rightly so. When she went to fetch their trays and drinks, Benjamin handed her his empty tea glass and demanded she refill it for him."

Buster questioned, "How did she react?"

Stein raised his eyebrows. "Oh, she was furious. But Benjamin managed to make it worse, of course. When she returned with just the food trays, he reproached her for not having his tea with her."

He shook his head. "Such a crude man."

Buster waited, but Stein seemed to lapse into deep thought. Buster tried to pull him back on track. "So, in the time you were sitting with him, he had already drank three glasses of tea?"

Stein glanced into Buster's eyes, and then seemed to be pondering his question. "Yes, I suppose so. Benjamin was very thirsty today."

"Was that unusual?"

Stein considered his question, "Perhaps. Benjamin always drank a lot of tea, but he may have been a little more obsessive today."

As Buster scribbled in his notebook, he asked, "What happened next?"

"Well, Ugidahli Unega came in ..."

Buster frowned. "Who?"

Stein smiled. "The Native American. He goes by White Feather."

Buster smiled and nodded grandly. "Oh, yes, of course. We've met."

Stein continued, "When Benjamin saw him, he patted his mouth, you know, and yelped like an Indian warrior, like kids do."

Buster shook his head. His uncle really was a crude man. No wonder he had plenty of enemies. "How did White Feather react?"

Stein smiled proudly. "He ignored him. White Feather never lets anyone get to him. He is a very strong man."

Buster agreed. He had found White Feather to be a remarkable person. Everyone in the sheriff's office that had worked with him on the Ludwig triple homicide investigation had been favorably impressed when he had come up with the solution independently. They had found him very wise and clever and respectful.

Buster noticed his good friend Birdie headed for the kitchen. He could tell from her demeanor that her interview with Agent Smiles had not gone well. She was walking fast, smoothing her dress and wearing a frown on a face that normally wore a bright and happy smile. He despised Smiles.

As he pulled out his notebook, he noticed that Birdie had stopped as she approached the double doors and was studying a shelf above the tea cart. She turned and looked around apparently searching for someone, spotted him, and waved him over.

"Excuse me, Albert, I'll be right back."

As he approached, she reached up, pulled a very dusty box from the shelf, blew the dust and wiped off the face of it, and started reading it. Buster looked over her shoulder. "What have you found?"

She looked at him with big eyes and a reassuring smirk. "Strychnine!"

Buster took out his handkerchief and took the box from Birdie, careful to avoid any spot that might have fingerprints. She pointed to the fine print at the bottom of a faded picture of an old barn with a giant rat in front of it. "Rodent Poison" was stamped in bold letters at an angle across the picture. "Contains Strychnine" was printed across the bottom of the box.

Buster looked up at the shelf and then down at the tea cart. "This was sitting up there?"

Birdie put her fists on her hips and nodded at him knowingly. "Mmm-hmmm."

Buster rotated the box. "Looks very old. How long has it been up there?"

Birdie held out her hands, "I guess forever. I never even noticed it until now and I pass by it every day." She laughed.

Buster glanced around the room. "So everyone had access to it?"

"Yessir."

Buster nodded, "OK, Birdie, good work."

Birdie shook her head and pushed through the double doors into the kitchen. Undersheriff Crab placed the box back on the shelf. The Crime Scene crew would want to see it. Buster motioned to Mr. Stein to stay put for a moment and found the sheriff to inform him of Birdie's find.

Chapter Thirteen
Finishing Up with Stein

When he returned, he found Mr. Stein sitting patiently with his legs crossed. Although he was Woody Allen's physical double, his disposition was that of a sophisticated and serious man. Buster sat down and apologized, "I'm sorry, Albert."

The patient man waved him off. Buster checked his notes and resumed with, "We were talking about White Feather. What happened next?"

Mr. Stein chuckled. "Mrs. Wilson returned with their teas and set Benjamin's just out of his reach and made him ask for it."

They both chuckled for a moment, then Stein continued, "Elizabeth was next."

The memory clearly disgusted him. He recrossed his legs and fidgeted. "When he spotted her, he sang that Lizzie Borden song."

Buster interrupted him, "Lizzie Borden song?"

Stein lowered his voice and sang it for the deputy. "Lizzie Borden took an ax and gave her father forty whacks. When the job was nicely done, she gave her mother forty-one."

He went on to explain, "It was from an old murder back in the 1890s ..."

Buster raised his hand. "Oh, yes, I remember hearing about it."

Stein took a deep breath. "It is particularly hurtful for Elizabeth since she was a resident here when it was the Colorado Institute for the Insane."

Buster glared at Stein. "She was?"

Stein nodded and continued as Buster made a note, "Elizabeth went into a rage and charged up to Benjamin. Several of her friends managed to hold her back, but she derided Benjamin warning him, and I quote, 'Keep it up, nigger, and one night they'll grab you around the neck and you won't know what's happening to you until they've strangled you to death!'"

Buster shifted in his chair and furrowed his brow. "Phew! Pretty strong words."

Stein raised his eyebrows and nodded. "Indeed. What made it even more macabre was Benjamin's convulsions made it appear that ghosts were indeed strangling him."

Buster was intrigued. "Tell me about the convulsions."

Stein shook his head. "Pretty scary. As I recall, Benjamin had complained about the taste of the tea to Birdie and she had brought him a new glass. He downed the whole glassful, and then vomited. He grabbed his throat and started flailing around. After several seconds, he dropped dead on the table."

Buster made a note and wrote "4" on his notepad and circled it. Then he probed, "He complained about the taste of the tea?"

Stein shifted in his seat and threw out his hands. "Yes, well, look, he complained about the taste of the food as well. I would not read too much into it. I think it was more to chide the cook and not a real problem with the tea. He drank every drop of the very tea he was criticizing. If the tea actually did taste strange, would he drink all of it?"

Buster nodded and rolled his head as if to concede the point. He reviewed his notes and circled the number he had written again. "So, Benny drank four glasses of tea given to him by four different sources?"

Albert Stein looked up and mouthed, "One, two, three, four."

He looked at the deputy and tilted his head. "Yes, I think so."

Buster glanced over his notes. "But, he reacted to the fourth glass of tea immediately?"

Stein studied the deputy as if seeking the meaning behind his question. "It would appear to be the straw that broke the camel's back."

Stein frowned and challenged the deputy, "Do you suspect foul play?"

Buster considered whether to share with the resident. But, of course, it would soon be common knowledge, "We think Benny may have been poisoned."

Stein looked down as if processing the information. Buster set down his notebook on his lap. "What was his relationship with Birdie?"

Stein was obviously irritated by the question. "Mrs. Beaudreau?"

Buster waited, Stein took a deep breath as if having to reach deep to tolerate this line of questioning. "LaWanda's heart is as big as ... well ..." he glanced at Buster to see if he got the metaphor, that LaWanda was a big woman. "She got along with Benjamin as well as anyone, with the exception of Katherine." Stein looked into Buster's eyes, "his girlfriend."

Buster frowned. "Katherine?" He checked his notes. "Would that be Katie Mae?"

Stein shrugged, nodded his head and rolled his hand as if to say "one and the same."

"When I was out here one time, the time he locked himself in his room, you said that Katie Mae was the only person that liked Benny. They still an item?"

Stein said, "Oh, yes."

Buster glanced across the room at the jovial, lovable cook consoling the St. Jude receptionist, his cousin, Naomi. In his mind, evidence was building against Birdie. She gave Benny the glass that seemed to have been fatal. Although she claimed to have just spotted the poison on the shelf by the kitchen after Benny's death, she might be covering, knowing that it would certainly be discovered anyway. Either way, she had access to the poison when she refilled his tea glass. But, then, so did everyone in the dining room.

Buster smiled at Albert, "Thank you, Albert, I don't have any more questions at this time."

Stein nodded. "I'll be around."

Chapter Fourteen
4:51 P.M. Frank's Testimony

"Hello, I'm Deputy Calhoun. I'd like to ask you a few questions." The thin deputy smugly flashed his badge as he pulled up a chair next to Franklin Roberts and flipped over a page of his notebook. Even though he looked nervous and unsure of himself, Frank sensed he was attempting to project an air of authority.

The deputy checked to make sure his body cam was turned on and began. "Your name?"

Frank looked at the large clock on the wall. He had been sitting in the dining room for over five hours. He was one of the last to be interviewed. He had watched the sheriff and his deputies interviewing the people in the dining room and had deduced that they did not have a system.

"Frank Roberts," he answered as he watched the crew that had been examining the crime scene carrying their bags and equipment out of the dining room. "Who's that?"

Startled, Calhoun spun back around. "Huh? Oh! Tha-that's CBI."

Frank frowned. "CBI?"

Calhoun puffed up and crossed his legs arrogantly. "C-B-I. That stands for Colorado Bureau of Insta ... uh, uh."

Frank guessed. "Investigation?"

Calhoun beamed. "Yeah. Investigation! Colorado Bureau of Investigators." Trying to regain his prestige, he added, "They come over from Springs and help us out. Wet Mountain County is too small for its own unit, you know."

Frank was getting tired and impatient. He tried to coax the deputy. "You wanted to ask me some questions?"

Deputy Calhoun shifted nervously. "Oh yes, uh, where were you when the victim died?"

Frank shrugged. "I was sitting next to him."

Calhoun's eyes bulged out. He looked around searching the room and then wrote hurriedly in his notebook. "How well did you know the deceased?"

Frank shifted in his chair. "I had just met him at lunch. His name is Benny, or Benjamin."

"Did you notice anything strange?"

"Well, I guess the whole meal was bizarre, especially the way he died."

Calhoun squinted. "The way he died?"

"It was as if some invisible person was strangling him and he was fighting to get free."

Calhoun withdrew his pencil, sat back in his chair and gave Frank a condescending look. "Invisible person?"

Frank nodded and then explained, "I know it sounds crazy, but that's what it looked like."

Calhoun eyed him for a moment, slowly nodding his head up and down as if doubtful. Frank looked down at his hands. Calhoun asked, "Know any VISIBLE people who might want to harm the victim?"

Images of TJ, the Wilsons, the cook, the Indian, and Albert flashed in his mind. "I only met him today. I don't hardly know anyone yet."

Calhoun was making notes as he asked, "Why's that?"

"I just moved in this morning."

Calhoun nodded and squinted as if scrutinizing him. "What's your room number?"

Frank wondered if he was a suspect. "I didn't know that the rooms have numbers."

Calhoun made a note, glanced over his notebook, then stuffed it in his shirt pocket. "OK, Mr. Roberts, that's all for now, but don't go anywhere."

Frank was confused, "You mean stay here in the dining room?"

Calhoun grinned, "Oh, no, I mean don't leave St. Jude, but you can go back to your room now."

Frank thanked him and stood. His knees popped and he felt very stiff. He stretched and managed to waddle out of the room to the elevator. He heard someone crying and looked over to see TJ being escorted by several men into the dining room. The poor teenager looked extremely upset.

Poor TJ, he thought as the elevator doors opened. Benny had probably stepped on a lot of toes with his belligerent personality. The sheriff and deputies would likely find a lot of suspects. He hoped TJ was not one of them.

He stepped into the elevator and selected "3." As the elevator bell dinged, announcing it was passing the second floor, Frank contemplated visiting Albert, but then decided he should not get involved. The bell dinged again and shuddered to a stop. The corridor and hallways that branched off it were empty. He hesitated at the door to his room. It was a nice room and St. Jude was a nice facility. It was so far removed from the box under the bridge he had called home for so long, he would not want to return to that life. But still, right now his new residence seemed small and depressing and the thought of returning to his new room left him feeling sad and alone.

Chapter Fifteen

5:30 P.M. Recapping on the Front Lawn

DEPUTY SAMUEL MORRISON STOOD quietly next to Undersheriff Buster Crab on the front lawn of the retirement center. Long shadows stretched across the clearing as the sun was dropping behind them above the Sangre de Cristo Mountains. Deputy Calhoun had ducked into the restroom for a pit stop. Sheriff Sean Bailey was still inside meeting with CBI's agent, Miles Blakeley.

Neither man noticed the scenery as they contemplated the apparent homicide. The investigators had diagnosed poisoning, probably strychnine. Buster broke the silence. "Birdie showed me a box of rat poison containing strychnine on a shelf near the kitchen doors and over the cart where glasses of tea had been poured. Everyone in the dining room had access to it."

Morrison shook his head. "Could've been anybody."

Buster blinked and looked at Morrison. He looked back at the distant Wet Mountains. Morrison studied his old friend and remembered that the victim was his uncle. "You alright, Buster?"

Buster breathed in deeply and shrugged. "Oh, yeah, tiring day."

Morrison agreed. "I'm sorry about your uncle."

"Uncle-in-law," Buster corrected. He glanced at Morrison. "Ellie, his wife, may have been the only person in the world that liked that old blowhard."

Morrison chuckled and pointed out, "Except, I guess he had a girlfriend at St. Jude."

Buster frowned at him. "A girlfriend at St. Jude?"

Morrison reminded him. "Mrs. Barkley said you heard giggling in his room when you went up to check on him."

Buster smiled. "Oh, yeah, that's right."

Then Buster got serious and reached for his notebook. "I'm gonna make a note. We need to look into that. Evidently, he trusted someone enough to let 'em bring him food."

Morrison smirked and made a note also. "You know anything about strychnine?"

Buster shrugged. "Not much. That box we found had strychnine in it."

Morrison nodded. Buster added, "Yeah, but you should've seen the dust on that box. It must've been sitting on that shelf for years. The picture and printing on the box looked like something from the forties."

Morrison shared, "I remember a case years back of a poisoning. We found rat poison under the sink but the medical examiner said it would've taken a lot more than what was missing from the box to kill a man."

"Did he say how much?"

Morrison tried to remember. "No, I don't think he said. And now that I think about it, it might not have even had strychnine in it. Seems like he told us that they had stopped putting strychnine in most rat poisons years ago."

Buster nodded. "We can ask when we get back. It's probably a controlled substance. Someone has bound to have been to a seminar."

Morrison pulled his notepad back out and made a note. Buster remarked, "Assuming the poison was delivered in his tea, there were at least four different people that refilled his tea and three had motives. There was the young girl, TJ, Mrs. Wilson and the cook, Birdie. I don't know who filled his first glass."

Morrison commented, "Hmm. Could've been in his food, I guess."

Buster added a note. "Yeah, possibly."

Morrison turned to his old friend, "Did you interview White Feather?"

The sheriff slipped up beside them and smiled broadly. "Yeah, I did."

Morrison nodded. "What was his take on it?"

Bailey laughed loudly. "Said he got what he had comin'."

Morrison laughed and shook his head. "White Feather doesn't pull any punches."

Bailey continued, "No, he doesn't. He had watched the table and pretty much backed up what others reported except he only saw Mrs. Wilson and Birdie bring him tea."

Morrison grinned slyly. "Did he see the spirits that were choking Benny?"

Bailey chuckled. "I didn't think to ask him. That would be a good question."

They laughed as Deputy Calhoun joined them. "What's so funny?"

The sheriff ignored him. Morrison explained, "We were wondering if White Feather might have been able to actually see the ghosts that murdered Mr. Cook."

Calhoun's eyes grew large. "Ghosts murdered Cook?"

Chapter Sixteen

6:28 P.M. Late for an Evening with Family

MORRISON CHECKED HIS WATCH as they pulled into the parking lot of the sheriff's office. "Crap!"

Calhoun was startled. "What? Whatsit?"

Morrison apologized. "Oh, sorry, Jessie. I just remembered that I was supposed to be over at Samantha's at six o'clock for dinner and a game of marbles."

Calhoun grinned. "Uh, oh."

"Yeah, I better call and explain."

Morrison felt the "butterflies" flooding into his stomach. Things had been going so well with his ex-wife and kids since he had moved to Rockcliffe. But he did not want to jeopardize it. He had a long way to go before their relationship was repaired.

Samantha had moved back to her hometown of Rockcliffe from Denver after the divorce. He feared it was probably to get away from him. He had been such an idiot, completely devoted to the Denver P. D. instead of his family. To block the pain, he had become even more devoted to his job and his over-zealousness had annoyed too many colleagues eventually leading to his boss letting him go on a trumped up charge of insubordination.

So when he accepted the deputy position in Rock-cliffe, he worried that Samantha would be furious. To his surprise, she had been very civil and had encouraged him to spend time with the kids.

As he walked to his car, he realized that he was exhausted and just wanted to crash into bed. He pulled out his cell phone and dropped into his car. "Hi, Sam, it's me. There's been a homicide out at St. Jude so I'm running late. Sorry."

Samantha seemed concerned. "Oh, dear! What happened?"

"Buster's uncle, Benjamin Cook, has been poisoned, we think. Unfortunately, everyone in the home had motive and opportunity, so we had to interview everyone."

"You must be exhausted."

What a wonderful woman. Morrison felt the weight start lifting from his shoulders. "Yeah, I am, actually."

"Want to reschedule?"

Morrison felt guilty. "I hate to. I'm sure you've gone to a lot of trouble ..."

"Oh, no, I just fixed some snacks and was going to grill some burgers when you got here. I can just throw everything into the frig for next time."

Next time, that sounded promising. "I really appreciate it, Sam. Tell the kids I'm sorry and I will make it up to them."

"Oh, it's really no problem, Sam. They have school tomorrow anyway."

As Morrison drove home to his small, two-bedroom townhouse, he felt a twinge of anxiety. Standing up her and the kids to work on a case was just the kind of thing that had led to their divorce. He had vowed to not let that happen again and, yet, here he was begging off an evening with the family because of a case.

Morrison tapped his forehead with his palm! Then he considered calling her back and ... no, it was too late.

Chapter Seventeen
Albert Stein Alone

ALBERT STEIN PAUSED AT his room door and glanced across the hallway at the door to Benjamin Cook's room. Poor Katherine. It was not completely true that she was the only person who liked Benjamin as he had told Buster. Truthfully, Albert did not dislike the contemptuous, egotistic rascal. He believed that Benjamin was actually a lonely, insecure man who acted up to cover his disappointment and feeling of failure and destitution.

Albert felt sorry for the desperate man who felt helpless and who feared that he had lost control of his life. Albert understood all too well what Benjamin was feeling. He suspected that most of the residents of St. Jude knew the feeling. They were in St. Jude because their lives had not worked out; they were destitute; time had run out on them. St. Jude was a home for those who had no other options. St. Jude was a place for people like him and Benjamin.

Most of the residents were grateful to St. Jude for giving them a shelter and food and a decent life, but they resented their situation and were bitter for what life had dealt them.

Albert stepped into his room and pushed the door closed. His corner room in the southwest corner of the second floor was, perhaps, the best room in the facility. He had a grand view of the back lawn, Sangre de Cristo Mountain range, and the southern sky. He walked across the room and rested his hands on the edge of the cabinet housing a sink. He looked into the mirror and studied his aged, wrinkled face and shriveled body. He needed a drink. He licked his dry lips and felt his stomach contract.

After Esther had died, he had turned to the bottle in the evenings. Evenings were the hardest time because that had been their time together. His old job as a newspaper reporter required long hours and often late nights. But no matter how tired he was or how devastated he was by the tragic events or disparaging stories he had to cover, Esther always had a way of perking him up and bringing him back to reality.

Esther was a wonderful woman who was comfortable in their simple life. She never seemed to mind that he did not make much money in his profession. It seemed to be enough for her that he enjoyed what he did and she seemed proud of him and his work.

She was steadfast in her faith, always ate kosher, was kind to all creatures. She had not deserved the curse of cancer. He should have been the one. He was the one that often abandoned his faith, ate bad food, ignored his health. He was the one that smoked and drank. He was the one that should have been destroyed by cancer, not Esther. Esther was pure.

Albert turned on the cold water and splashed his grimy face. He reached for a towel and scrubbed his face as if trying to scrub away his memories as well. He reached down and opened the small apartment-sized refrigerator and pulled out a Dr. Pepper. He turned to the sweet soda pop in hopes that it would drive away his thirst for whiskey. It never did, but he needed something to get him through the evening.

As he dropped into the recliner, Albert's eyes were drawn to the objects hanging on the walls. Pitiful objects to remind him of his inconsequential life. The old type-set drawer filled with typeset letters hung like a shadow box. It had once hung in the corner of the living room above his desk and typewriter. He had picked it up out of the trash behind the Denver Post building. It had been thrown out when the new digital equipment had replaced the antiquated typesetting machines. He felt like the drawer, old and obsolete.

Next to the drawer, an award-winning article he wrote on the closing of the Colorado Institute for the Insane, was yellowing in a cheap frame. It had seemed appropriate since the building that had been built for the insane was now St. Jude Methodist Center for the Indigent. He had won numerous awards over the years but most of them were stuffed in an old chest somewhere. They were probably in the dusty basement of St. Jude, lost and forgotten like the ghosts of time past.

An amateurish painting of Esther hung on the wall across from the foot of his bed. It had been painted by Esther's aunt and although it fell dreadfully short of capturing her likeness, Esther had bragged on it and proudly kept it hanging prominently in the living room for all to see. She always pointed it out to guests and exclaimed how proud she was to have such a talented aunt.

He wondered if her love for her aunt clouded her vision and in it she saw what her aunt saw in her mind's eye. He wondered if she really thought it was good or just pretended to like it. Or maybe it was for her what it was for him now—something he liked only because she liked it. And it reminded him of her unselfish love.

Albert picked up the remote control from its spot on the arm of the chair, pointed it at the small TV and pressed the power button. It was time for national news. It was time to endure the pitiful state to which journalism had descended.

Chapter Eighteen
The Black Firebird

MORRISON JUST WANTED TO throw off his clothes and go to bed but forced himself to take a shower. His body was tired, but his mind was in high gear feasting on the tasty morsels of clues from the day's interviews. He knew that if he went straight to bed, he would just toss and turn until his mind caught up with his body.

The hot shower temporarily rejuvenated him and stimulated his mind. Birdie would have to be the prime suspect at this point since she delivered the glass of tea that appeared to have triggered Cook's convulsions. The weird, wild woman, Lizzie Dawson would also merit closer examination. She seemed to have a visceral dislike for the victim. The poison on the shelf was uniquely convenient, but it was in such plain sight that if someone accessed it, it should have attracted the attention of anyone nearby. Plus, the dust on the box suggested that Birdie was the first person in maybe decades that had touched it. He reasoned that strychnine most likely had a shelf life and surely would be weakened by now.

Living alone, Morrison had long since dropped the formalities of wearing a robe or underwear from the bathroom to the bedroom. As he stepped out of the steamy bathroom, the frosty air chilled his naked body. Originally, he was just going straight to bed after the shower, but now he had a burst of energy and decided to grab his robe and go downstairs for a snack.

He glanced at his watch. It was a few minutes past seven. As he approached the closet, car lights lit up the window and he heard the low rumble of a big engine idling down. The car was stopping in front of his townhouse. He altered his course to peek through the shades and saw a black car with a large golden firebird painted on the hood. "Oh, no!"

As the car door opened, his mind raced through his options. Was the front door locked? Did he have time to grab his pistol or his robe?

A woman with long dark hair stepped out of the car. The woman was all too familiar. *Darla! The waitress at Maggie's restaurant.*

When he had first met her, he had found her to be shy and reserved. She had seemed so withdrawn and homely, that he had felt sorry for her. But, it was during his first murder investigation in Rockcliffe that things got out of control.

Jon Ludwig, a Wet Mountain County deputy, his wife and son were found murdered in their house. Ludwig fancied himself a photographer and had used his camera to photograph crime scenes. But, they would learn that he had also used his camera to acquire incriminating pictures of colleagues and citizens to use for blackmail.

They had found nude pictures of Darla and learned that she was Ludwig's mistress. Feeling sorry for her, the sheriff and he had decided to give her the pictures and keep the affair quiet. Unexpectedly, Darla had been very appreciative and had turned her attention and affection toward him. He had already had a close call when she had surprised him at his motel room before he had gotten the townhouse. Fortunately, that time he had been saved by a call from dispatch.

He feared that if the front door was unlocked, she might let herself in as she had done at the motel. With no time for the robe and no need for the pistol, Morrison raced down the stairs to try to beat her to the door. Just as he reached the bottom of the stairs, two steps from the door, it opened. He ducked behind the door, flattened out against the wall and listened as Darla stepped calmly onto the linoleum square in front of the door, stopped and called out, "Sam? Are you home?"

He was trapped! He heard her step off the linoleum onto the carpet and caught glimpses of her from behind the door as she boldly headed upstairs. "Sam? Sam? I'm coming up."

Stealthily, he slipped from behind the door and tiptoed into the living room and out of sight of the dauntless woman. He glanced around looking for something to cover up with. He found an apron in the kitchen and slipped out the back door onto the concrete patio in the tiny backyard. Maybe he could hide in the detached garage.

As he paused at the edge of the small concrete patio, he glanced up at the window of the small second bedroom. Darla would have had time to search the master bedroom and bathroom. If she searched the second bedroom, she might look out the window and see him. He decided to make a dash for the garage.

The tall weeds hid the goat-head vines growing underneath. The goat-heads stung the bottoms of his feet and he yelped and tried to brush them off quickly as he reached the door of the garage.

He paused to check the window of the second bedroom. No one was there. But as he exhaled in relief, he saw her standing behind the sliding glass door of the dining room on the ground floor laughing at him. He straightened the skimpy apron and glared at her hoping she would get his message of rejection. But his misery seemed to inspire her. Her laughter turned into a seductive smirk as she sashayed across the dining room to the back door in the kitchen.

His feet were stinging from the goat-heads; his bare skin felt as though it were icing over; and his heart was racing as the beguiling woman opened the back door and stepped onto the patio. "There you are," she declared.

Morrison turned and threw open the garage door, stepped in and swiped off goat-heads from the bottom of his feet, slammed the door and locked it. The concrete floor was freezing. He was freezing. Now what would he do?

He could get into his car, but he had no keys. He heard Darla trying the door knob. "Sam?"

"Go away!" he demanded.

"Sam," she scolded in a low, sultry voice, "let me in, Sam."

Morrison glanced around the garage desperately searching for something, anything, to wear. He spotted an old pair of greasy coveralls hanging on the wall. They were remnants from the previous owner. He shivered at the thought of pulling them on over his bare body, but he was freezing.

As he zipped up the thick coveralls, he realized that Darla had been very quiet. Suddenly, the back door to the garage flew open and the sultry woman stepped in. She stopped, covered her mouth and protested, "Oh! What happened to your sexy apron?"

Feeling more confident in coveralls, he straightened up and used his most authoritative voice to declare, "Darla, this has to stop. I apologize if I have given you the wrong impression, but ..."

As he spoke, Darla approached him confidently and started pulling off her fur coat. Morrison grabbed the lapels and closed the coat back across her, "Alright, you leave me no choice. Darla, I am arresting you for trespassing."

Darla smiled brightly and leaned against him. "OOO! Are you going to handcuff me?"

Morrison pushed her toward the door prompting her to giggle. "Oh! You want to play rough?"

"No, Darla, I don't want to play at all. Don't you understand? I Don't want to have anything to do with you."

He dragged her through the front door of the garage and stepped onto the bed of goat-heads. "Ow! Ouch!"

He let go of her arm and tried to swipe the bottoms of his feet. Darla took advantage of her freedom to walk to the patio, turn and stare at him sadly, turn back and enter the house.

Morrison watched her stop and wave at him from the dining room and then leave. He tried to walk on his heels to help limit the awful stickers to the balls and toes of his feet. Not knowing what he would find inside, he swiped the bottoms of his feet, and tentatively ventured through the dark kitchen, and crossed through the dining room into the living room. Expecting the persistent woman to appear from the shadows, he strained to search the dark room but found it empty.

He heard the deep rumble of her car starting, then the thundering roar of the big engine. He pulled back the heavy living room drapes and peeked out. To his relief, the black Firebird was gone.

He locked the front door and peeled off the disgusting coveralls, then headed upstairs for another shower. He wondered if the neighbors had seen his sexy visitor. *Would news get back to Samantha?* All of the progress that had been made patching things up since he had moved to Rockcliffe could all go up in smoke thanks to Darla.

Monday

Chapter Nineteen
Deedie's Reproach/Reviewing Reports

It was a chilly, but refreshing morning and Deputy Sam Morrison was eager to get to work. Life was good. He was liking his job with the Wet Mountain County Sheriff's Office much more than he had expected he would. Today the feelings of rejection, humiliation, and betrayal that he had felt when he was fired from his detective position in Denver were gone.

People were so friendly and accepting in the small town that he had regained his self-esteem. They had made him feel human again. Morrison threw open the back door and strode through the hallway past the laundry room and kitchen area of detention. He turned down the short hallway and quickly found the breakroom in the corner of the big open area of the offices.

After pouring his coffee, he crossed the open area and found Deedie in dispatch with her nose behind a paperback, as usual. "Whatcha readin' today?"

Without blinking, Deedie responded, "Agatha Christopher."

Morrison strolled up to the small desk. "Oh, yeah, the local mystery writer, not the British author, right?"

Deedie did not respond. Morrison tried to make a joke. "She's the one that wrote *Murder on the Royal Gorge Express, right?*"

Deedie frowned and rolled her eyes in the manner that teenagers show older people their disgust for their humor. Morrison tried to chuckle, but for some reason her cold reproach hurt him. Perhaps, the put-down reminded him that he was no longer young and attractive to pretty young girls. In her eyes, he was old, boring, and ridiculous.

The wounded deputy slinked away, back into the offices. He would turn his mind to the homicide and the reports he needed to type up.

He found his old friend, Buster Crab, in the break room stirring his coffee. "Good morning, Chief."

Buster's official title was undersheriff, but around the office he was just "Chief." He was so deep in thought he did not seem to hear his old friend. Buster had also worked for the Denver Police Department. Buster had worked in the burglary division and they had met while working a case that overlapped. Through the years, they had become close friends. Morrison refilled his cup with the strong, black brew. Buster had not moved. "You alright, Buster?"

Buster seemed startled by his question. "Huh? Oh, yeah," he chuckled, "Sorry, Sam. I guess I was a million miles away."

Morrison shrugged. "That's alright. I didn't mean to startle you."

The reflective undersheriff appeared to be returning to his thoughts and then explained, "I was just thinking about my aunt Ellie and how she put up with Benny all those years. I just wonder how she did it. Then I got to thinking about him having a new girlfriend."

Buster shrugged and grinned. "How can a man like that be so attractive to women?"

Morrison chuckled. Buster remarked, "How does a man like that rate a sweet, loving, loyal wife like Ellie?"

Morrison shook his head. He made a good point. "There's just no explaining love ... or the female heart for that matter."

Buster nodded and headed for his office. "You're right about that."

Morrison headed for the shared desks where his skinny partner was busy typing. When he heard Morrison pull back a chair, Calhoun stopped typing and smirked. "Did she forgive you?"

Morrison frowned and then remembered their discussion the night before. "Oh, yeah, it was no problem."

Calhoun crossed his arms, sat back in the chair and kicked his feet up on the desk. "You're pretty lucky."

Morrison turned on his computer and waited for it to boot up. He did not feel much like talking or explaining how wonderful his ex-wife was to his nosy colleague. Calhoun took a deep breath, looked up at the ceiling and put on a look of authority. "Most women get all upset when you stand 'em up. They don't understand the demands on law enforcement officers. They think they should be the only thing in your life."

Calhoun glanced at Morrison to get his reaction. Morrison ignored him as he logged into his computer.

Calhoun continued, "I guess Samantha is different. She was married to you for all those years, so she knows how things come up and you have to respond. She knows how the family has to take a backseat sometimes."

Morrison felt his face getting hot. Samantha HAD been through it before. His dedication to the job and putting the family second was the reason she had divorced him. Now, just as he was making some headway restoring their relationship, he had put her second again. Suddenly, his stomach contracted and he felt anxious. *How much damage had last night caused? Did she really understand or was she privately thinking "here we go again." Is she thinking that I haven't changed?*

"I gotta get my notes typed up," He barked.

Calhoun removed his feet off the desk and headed for dispatch to flirt with Deedie. And now the image of Darla stalking him at his townhouse flashed into his mind and filled his heart with panic.

Deputies Morrison and Calhoun, and Chief Crab spent the morning typing up and then reviewing their interviews from St. Jude. Morrison suggested that they sort the reports into stacks: based on "suspects," "persons of interest," and "probably innocent." Since everyone at St. Jude had motive (they all hated Benjamin Cook) and opportunity, the task was very difficult. But, Morrison had done it many times and guided his colleagues through the process.

Based upon the reports, the prime suspects included LaWanda "Birdie" Beaudreau, TJ Holloway, Elizabeth "Lizzie" Dawson, Mrs. Benaford Wilson, and Albert Stein.

Persons of interest included White Feather, Frank Roberts, and Elizabeth's friends, Lucy, Ruth, Mary, and Benny's girlfriend, Katherine "Katie" Mae.

It became clear to Morrison as they reviewed the reports, that Calhoun, and to some extent Crab and the Sheriff, were not expert interviewers. So, he made a list of people he wanted to re-interview.

Then Morrison recommended they put up a large white board to work from. The sheriff agreed with the request, but since Wet Mountain County had a small budget, he suggested they make do with a large cork board he had seen stored in the shed behind the office until they could afford to order a white board.

Twenty

7:02 A.M. Stacie's Tour

IT WAS THE SECOND knock, knock, knock that caught Frank's attention. It took him a minute to realize that he was in a bed and in a room with walls and a door instead of the cardboard box he had lived in for so many years. No one ever knocked on his box under the bridge to wake him.

He managed a groggy "come in" and the door opened. He sat up and pivoted to sit on the side of his bed covering his lap with the sheet. He rubbed his eyes and strained to look at the pretty young aid standing just inside the door. "Who are you?" he asked.

"Good morning, Mr. Roberts, I'm Stacie. I work the night shift. How are you this morning? Sleep well?"

Frank looked around as if trying to get his bearings, then slumped. "I slept alright, I guess."

He watched the young, twenty-ish aid buzz around his room, pulling out drawers, laying out clothes. "You dress all the residents?"

Stacie stopped and laughed. Then she straightened up and turned. "Oh! No. I'm sorry, Mr. Roberts. I was just ... ," she waved her hand across the collection of clothes.

Frank smiled. "It's no problem, I just haven't had anyone ... well, you know."

Stacie smiled brightly. She had a beautiful smile, he
thought. He felt a little awkward since he had slept in the
nude. Something he had not done since he had moved
into his cardboard box under the bridge. The clean sheets
and warm room had reminded him of those days when
he always undressed for bed; those days before he had
lost everything and had been forced to join the ranks of
the homeless. But, now, with the pretty young woman
in the room, he felt confined to his bed and the cover of
his sheet. "I would get up, but ... well ..." He looked down
and Stacie got it.

"Oh!" she shrieked. "Let me leave you to ..." She
stopped at the door. "I'll be right back. This is your first
day and I am supposed to go over some stuff with you."

She grabbed the door knob and stared out. "Say,
fifteen minutes?"

"That should be enough time."

She closed the door behind her and he slipped off the
bed and snatched some underwear on his way to the
bathroom. He started to lock the door to Ralph's room
and then decided not to.

After relieving himself and brushing his teeth, he
dressed in the shirt and pants Stacie had picked out for
him. He sat down on the soft, but worn recliner, picked
up a pair of socks and smelled of them. Wearing fresh
clothes every day would take some getting used to.

He leaned back in the recliner and sucked in to
refresh his lungs. Putting on socks was more difficult than
he remembered. He realized he had slept through the
night; he had been warm all night; he had not worried

about a coyote or a bear slipping up to investigate his cardboard domicile. He heard a soft knock on the door. "Come in."

The door opened slowly and Stacie peeked around. "Oh, good, you're dressed."

She pushed the door open and stepped in cradling a clipboard against her chest. "Shall we get the paperwork done first?"

"Sounds good."

Stacie wiggled up onto the bed and pulled a pencil from behind her ear. "First, the rules." She tilted her head to one side and made a sad face, "I'm afraid there's a bunch of them. I'm sorry."

Stacie looked up from the clipboard. "And finally, there are two elevators. One has red doors and one has silver doors. Residents are only allowed to use the silver doors. Red doors are reserved for staff."

She boldly checked it off her list and dropped the clipboard onto her lap, "OK? Any questions?"

Frank joked, "Oh, I'm sorry, were you talking to me?"

Stacie's eyes got wide and then she squinted, pursed her lips and pointed a wriggling finger at him. "Alright, you!"

She giggled and hopped off the bed. "I'll need your autograph."

Frank signed the form and she moved that page to the back of the stack. "OK, now for your room orientation."

She led him around his room pointing out the thermostat, the bed crank, the lever on the recliner, the lock on the door. She noticed his makeshift calendar and explained proudly that he could hang anything he wanted on the walls but should call maintenance to do the work.

Then they went into the bathroom and she pointed out Ralph's door and the lock and explained etiquette, "You may lock it while you are using the facilities, but don't forget to unlock it."

Frank informed her of how he had already learned that lesson and of Ralph's visit. She giggled. "Well, at least you got to meet your neighbor."

She went on to explain that the window was nailed shut and was not to be opened. She pointed out the heater and explained how to work it. She explained how to operate the shower. She pointed out which drawer and cabinet below the lavatory was his and then smiled as she checked off the last item on the Room Orientation list.

She raised her eyebrows and smiled at him and asked, "Any questions?"

Frank smiled. "Seems clear enough."

Stacie turned and led him back through his room. Then they headed down the wide corridor to the parlor that was next door to his room. "The parlor," she said as she gestured with her hand. He followed her into the room as she gestured to the right pointing out the large, flat screen TV that was mounted on the wall with a short bookcase below filled with movie DVDs and the remote control. Comfortable looking Victorian-style chairs and a couch faced the TV, arranged theater style.

The left side of the room was set up as a library. Floor-to-ceiling book cases lined the walls filled with books, paperbacks and magazines. In the northeast corner, the wall curved out to form a semi-circular alcove with large windows looking out over the front lawn. It was set up like a cozy reading area complete with a couch and a chair with an ottoman.

"Very nice," Frank commented. He was enjoying Stacie's enthusiastic tour and decided not to tell her that Mrs. Barkley had already shown him the common areas.

The tour wound up conveniently in time for breakfast on the first floor. Stacie looked at her watch and proclaimed, "Well! Any questions?"

Frank smiled. "Thank you, Stacie, it was lovely."

He felt his face flush from his comment that sounded more like the end of a date rather than the end of a tour. Stacie brushed his arm with her hand. "Your welcome. Well, it's time for me to go to school. I'll see you tonight."

Frank grimaced. "School?"

Stacie beamed. "I'm taking some courses at CSU in Pueblo."

Frank marveled at her initiative. "Don't you ever sleep?"

Stacie put a finger to her lips. "Shh. Don't tell anybody, but I sleep on the job!"

Frank shared a good laugh with the delightful girl. She patted his arm and rushed off. Frank turned to enter the dining room and then paused. "The crime scene," he muttered.

Chapter Twenty-One

8:05 A.M. New Friends, Life Is Good

THIS EARLY IN THE morning, only a few residents were clustered around the several tables for breakfast. Frank looked for a familiar face. He recognized Lizzie and her friends quietly eating at their same table. The other residents were strangers. He felt a hand on his shoulder.

"Good morning, Franklin." Albert Stein stood beside him and offered his hand as if passing a secret note.

Frank shook his hand and smiled. "Good morning, Albert."

Stein scanned the mostly empty tables. "Shall we try a different table this morning?"

Frank chuckled. "Let's."

Stein led his friend to the area in front of the kitchen where steaming pans were set up buffet style, handed him a plate and fell in behind him. It was a great spread featuring scrambled eggs, bacon, sausage, buttered toast, French toast and assorted fruit. Nothing like the grub he had waited in long lines for at the soup kitchens and shelters back in Canon City.

The drink carts featured a choice of coffee, orange or apple juice. Stein stepped up and glanced at his new friend. "That pitcher by the coffee is milk."

Frank smiled graciously. "You remembered. Thanks."

As they walked past the infamous table where Benny had held court, they paused to note the chalk line on the floor and the yellow "crime scene" tape encircling the table. Albert appeared sad as he surveyed the table and then moved on. Frank followed him to a nice table next to the tall, wide windows that looked out over the back lawn and pond. The barren peaks on the massive mountains of the Sangre de Christos were a majestic backdrop to the spectacular view that took his breath away. He stood for a moment to admire it.

Albert interrupted his trance. "Wait until you see them with their snow caps."

Frank turned, set his tray down on the large, oval-shaped table and joined his friend. "How do you get used to that?"

Albert looked and nodded. "It is impressive isn't it? Perhaps later we should go for a walk to see the grounds."

Frank raised his eyebrows. "That'd be great."

Frank had just taken his first bite when Albert announced, "Good morning, Rudolph. Mind if we're sitting at your table this morning?"

Frank looked up and recognizing the grumpy, wrinkled face of his next door neighbor. Ralph recognized him. "Oh, it's you."

Frank smiled and managed to swallow his mouthful of eggs. He greeted him warmly, "Good morning, neighbor."

Albert glanced at Frank. "So, you've met?"

Ralph raised his eyebrows as he dumped his silverware out of his napkin, "Locked me out of the bathroom."

Albert chuckled. A stooped old man in a red plaid shirt and jeans slipped quietly by Albert and chose a spot with space between him, Albert and Ralph. As he silently placed his tray on the table, Frank recognized the tuft of hair splaying up through a hollowed out deer leg bone and the white owl feather dangling on one side of his face. Albert handled introductions, "Franklin Roberts meet Ugidahli Unega."

Ralph looked surprised. "Who?"

The old Cherokee turned to Frank and introduced himself, "Just call me White Feather."

Frank nodded. "Just call me Frank."

Frank was anxious to make friends. "So, what does it mean?"

The old men looked at him curiously, as Frank tried to pronounce what he had heard, "OOgee-dolly ...?"

White Feather chuckled; Albert repeated the Indian's name. "Ugidahli Unega."

White Feather translated, "It means White Feather."

Albert added, "He's Cherokee."

Frank and Albert laughed; Ralph was disinterested.

Frank tried to change the subject. "So, how long have you been here?"

White Feather did not respond. Frank reasoned that people at St. Jude might be reluctant to talk about their past. He knew he was. So, he changed the subject again. "We sure have spectacular views."

Ralph ignored the rookie and addressed Albert, "Glad to be rid of that blowhard?"

Albert paused and glanced at the table where Benny loved to sit. "Benjamin was a very troubled man."

Ralph scooped up eggs on his fork. "Is that what he was?"

White Feather cautioned as he continued to eat. "Do not speak the name of the dead."

Ralph set down his fork and glared at the old medicine man, "Why's that?"

White Feather paused and looked into his eyes. "His soul is searching for his ancestors in the Nightland. Saying his name will call him back from his journey."

Ralph stared at the old sage, and then picked up his fork to resume eating. "I expect that soul is roasting over an open fire right now."

Everyone laughed, even White Feather. Frank was smiling inside as he enjoyed a good meal, a warm and comfortable shelter, a beautiful view, and new friends. Life was good.

A tall, portly man with a round, baby face and happy, dancing eyes appeared and set his tray down next to Ralph. "I say! Jolly good morning, eh?"

Albert answered for everyone. "Good morning, Walter."

Albert looked at Frank. "Have you met Walter, Franklin?"

Frank stood and reached out his hand. "Frank."

Walter's eyes brightened, huffed in a stuttering sort of way, and reached out his hand, "G-good to m-meet you, F-Frank. Just call me Monty."

Then he chuckled like an old British aristocrat from a movie. Frank tried to place the character. As Monty sat down and cleared his throat again in a stuttering sort of way, Frank remembered—Dr. Watson from the Sherlock Holmes movies. Frank chuckled to himself; the resemblance was uncanny. He looked to Albert, then Ralph, then Monty. He was surrounded by celebrities—Woody Allen, Walter Mathau, and Nigel Bruce. Then he looked at White Feather. There was only one White Feather; he was an original. He wondered what actor they might associate with him. Basil Rathbone? White Feather had the poise and confidence, but was not nearly as outgoing and dominant.

He shook his head. It had occurred to him before, but he had never discussed it with anyone else. He inquired, "Have you ever noticed that the older you get, the more people look like someone else you know?"

Ralph ignored him and White Feather just closed his eyes. Walter seemed confused, but Albert had a thoughtful response. "Perhaps it is because there are only a finite number of original families."

Ralph frowned at him. "Original families?"

Albert tried to explain. "We are all descendants of the original families of man. I suspect that those family traits are replicated with each generation."

Walter's eyes sparkled as he seemed to get it, but Ralph seemed disgusted by the whole thing. Albert was curious. "What do you think, Ugidahli?"

White Feather opened his eyes and studied Albert for a moment. His response was a simple nod. But Frank was impressed. "I think you've hit on it, Albert. I think you must be exactly correct."

Monty raised his eyebrows as he flicked his cloth napkin and placed it on his lap. "Any n-news on ..." he pointed toward the table wrapped in yellow tape.

Ralph and White Feather ignored him and continued to eat. Albert smiled. "Did you hear that they suspect poison?"

That caught Ralph and White Feather's attention, Monty glanced about nervously. "You don't say?"

"Probably strychnine," Albert added.

"Where do you get strychnine?" Ralph grumbled.

He was startled by Birdie putting her hand on his shoulder causing him to dump his fork load of eggs into his lap. The large woman shook with laughter and then while he scraped up the mess, she explained, "I found a box of rat poison on that old dusty shelf above the tea tray. It has strychnine in it."

In unison the five elderly friends turned to search for the mysterious shelf. They gasped In unison when they located the unassuming shelf supporting cereal box sized boxes and odd antique metal utensils.

"Son of a gun!" Ralph commented, "Never noticed that before."

Then Albert remembered. "That's what you showed Undersheriff Crab."

Birdie grinned proudly. "You bet I did and they's perty intrested in it, too."

Albert smiled. "Yes, I bet so."

Chapter Twenty-Two

10:02 A.M. The Cork Board

MORRISON AND CALHOUN FOUND the large cork board
that Sheriff Bailey recommended in the shed and had set
it up on a wall in the office open area. Down the left side
now was the timeline for the times leading up to and just
after the death of Benjamin Cook. Pictures of the many
suspects were pinned across the top.

Sheriff Bailey strolled up holding his extra-large bever-
age cooler filled with tea. He stopped and studied the
board. Morrison and Calhoun backed up to stand beside
him and wait for his reaction. Deputy Melton watched
from his desk.

Bailey beamed. "Uptown!"

Everyone kept studying the board. Bailey shook his
head. "Plenty of suspects."

Morrison nodded in agreement and then remembered.
"Buster suggested there might be someone in the office
that could tell us something about strychnine."

Bailey raised his eyebrows and then muttered, "I'll
bet Bobby knows something. He looked into the office of

the administrative assistant. "Kathy would you check to see if Bobby's in today?"

Bobby Goodnight was a big, barrel-chested man with a round, baby face and commanding presence. Close inspection revealed that he was older than he looked, but still only thirty-one. He barged into the room and blasted out, "Hey, Sheriff, what'dya need?"

Bailey smiled and answered softly, "Hey, Bobby, we were wondering what you know about strychnine."

Bobby shrugged. "What do you want to know about it?"

Bailey nodded to Morrison. "How long would it take for a man to feel the effects of strychnine poisoning?"

Bobby took a deep breath. "That what killed Buster's uncle?"

Bailey intercepted the question. "We think it might be."

Bobby shrugged. "Really depends upon the dosage and the size of the man, but I would say as little as ten minutes, as long as two hours."

Morrison asked, "Any idea what the shelf life might be?"

Bobby's eyes bulged and his cheeks puffed out as he exhaled. "Oh, boy. Practically forever. I would say a hunnerd years, maybe?"

Everyone got quiet while processing this revelation. Bobby asked, "Why? You think the poison was old?"

Bailey explained, "We found a box of rat poison that had strychnine in it. No telling how old it was. We figure it might be from the forties or fifties."

Bobby poked out his lower lip. "Sixty years old? Might still pack a wallop. Would probably take a large dose, though."

Morrison expelled his disappointment with his breath.

Calhoun swelled up, adjusted his heavy utility belt, and threw in his theory. "Well, the way I see it, we've got three primary suspects. We know three people who had access to the victim's tea glass—TJ, Mrs. Wilson, and Birdie, the cook."

He ignored the perturbed looks of his colleagues as he proudly strolled up to the board and pointed to the picture of a young girl with a bright smile. "Now, let's look at TJ Holloway—a young, aspiring girl working and going to school. She loved her job, loved the residents. Then one day a big, scary bully shows up. He makes her job a living hell. She complains, but nothing happens.

"So, that day when he touches her inappropriately, she snaps like a dry twig. She goes over to the tea cart and looks up and sees the dusty old brown box. It says rat poison and she thinks, 'I'll fix him.' She pictures him getting real sick. She doesn't know that long ago, they put strychnine in rat poison and that it can kill him. So, she's driving home and gets the call that Mr. Cook is dead! She is devastated. That is why she was so upset when she was brought back in, don't you see?"

Calhoun turned around to find himself alone. The sheriff was in his office doing paperwork; Bobby Goodnight had disappeared; Melton was sitting in a chair leaning back against the wall asleep; and Morrison had his feet propped up on a desk staring at him. Calhoun's eyes widened and his chest deflated like a punctured balloon. Embarrassed and humiliated, he dragged himself back to a desk and sat down. As he nervously straightened first one stack of papers then another, Morrison offered, "Interesting Hypothesis."

Calhoun continued to tidy things up on the desk and tried to act like it was no big deal. But Morrison felt sorry for his flustered friend and asked, "What's your take on Mrs. Wilson?"

Calhoun shrugged and fidgeted in his chair for a moment and then answered, "Well, Mrs. Wilson is a strong woman, a very strong woman. And, she is very protective of Mr. Wilson."

He looked at Morrison and whispered, "He has Alzheimer's, you know."

Morrison nodded. Calhoun continued, "She had ample opportunity to poison his tea. And, she had ample motive. She despised Mr. Cook."

He raised his eyebrows. "That leaves Birdie, the cook. She's the only one that had access to both his tea AND his food."

Morrison nodded, put his finger beside his mouth and thumb under his chin and inquired, "So, do you have a favorite?"

Calhoun looked confused. Morrison smiled. "Are you leaning toward one more than the others?"

Calhoun swelled up and propped his feet up on the desk. "I want to see the lab report. If his food was poisoned, well, then I'd say the cook did it!"

Chapter Twenty-Three

12:50 P.M. First Encounter with Nurse Nujent

Frank was chewing his last bite of toast when he felt everything get quiet and still. He stopped chewing and glanced around the table. His new friends were staring behind him. He turned to find a short, stern lady with short black hair glaring at him with dark eyes. Frank was startled by her ominous appearance. "Mr. Roberts, are you ready for your examination?"

Albert frowned and interceded. "Oh, good morning, Nurse Nujent. Frank, have you met our resident nurse?"

Frank downed his milk and stood. "It is a pleasure to meet you, Ms. Nujent. I was very impressed with your efforts to save Mr. Cook yesterday."

She glared at him, nodded with a smirk on her lips as if to say "oh, sure," turned and stomped off. Frank glanced at Albert who shrugged and whispered direly, "Good luck, Franklin."

Ralph added, "You'll need it."

The infirmary was on the north end of the ground floor. There was an examining room connecting to an office/pharmacy that connected to a clinic/storeroom. Nujent commanded him to sit on the examining table, shoved a clipboard into his chest and handed him a pencil. "Fill that out. Fill it all out. Be thorough."

She marched into her office before he could answer.

It was the most comprehensive medical questionnaire he had ever filled out. He could hear the grumpy woman stirring in her office and wanted to peek in the door, but resisted. He did not want to get on her bad side, so, finished, he set down the clipboard and let his eyes explore the room.

He chuckled to himself as he thought, *not exactly eye-candy.* The walls were bare, furniture was sparse, containers and equipment neatly placed. Frank had a mischievous urge. He slipped off the examining table and swapped two identical containers on a nearby table then quietly returned to the examining table.

Nurse Nujent burst into the room. "You done yet?"

Frank responded by handing her the clipboard. She snatched it out of his hand and started going over it, flipping the pages angrily. "You haven't checked off any maladies."

Frank shrugged. "Don't have any."

Nujent glared at him with her lips pressed tightly and her temples rippling. "What medications are you taking?"

Frank calmly answered, "Don't take any."

She turned her head slightly to one side and glared at him for a moment. He sensed he was on her bad side now. She handed him the clipboard and angrily said, "Sign it!"

He turned to the last page and saw his signature. He tried to hand it back. "I did sign it."

"Sign every page!" she demanded.

He was surprised to find that there was a place on every page for his signature. As he signed each page, Nujent walked over to the table where he had swapped the containers. She paused and studied them for a moment, lifted the lid on one, then slowly, she turned and glared at him. He kept his eyes trained on the clipboard. She swapped the containers back, slamming them down to purposefully make a sound with her eyes trained on him.

Frank tried to look innocent. He handed the clipboard back and smiled. She snatched the clipboard. "Take off your shirt."

He took off his shirt and tried to keep a cheerful countenance as she roughly took his blood pressure, checked his heart, and all the other trivial things that make up a "thorough" examination.

When she dismissed him, she gave him a wary look. "I'm keeping an eye on you, Roberts."

Frank smiled. "That's very kind of you, Ms. Nujent, but I wouldn't want any special treatment."

"Hmmph."

Chapter Twenty-Four

10:11 A.M. New Friends in New Places

It was the first time Frank had noticed something smelling stronger than himself in years. When the elevator doors closed, he noticed a stale smell somewhat covered by a familiar Lysol smell. He smiled proudly, happy that he smelled fresher than his surroundings.

Frank was just naturally reluctant to meet new people, but he was always curious about the workings of things. So, he decided to check out the common areas of his new home. A bell dinged softly, the elevator lurched, there was a long pause and then the doors opened. He was on the second floor where the corridor was filled with echoes of voices and television. He exited to his right where the first common area was a large, empty, dark room with a sign above the door reading "Activity/Hobby Room." Across the corridor was a room labeled "Parlor" that was very similar to the parlor on his floor except it was all library and no television. He peeked in to see an elderly lady in a wheel chair asleep in the corner and a man reading in the alcove.

The noise was coming from the room on the opposite side of the corridor, the room labeled simply "Recreation." Inside, men were gathered around the pool tables, and in the back, the ladies were sitting in tall-backed chairs watching *Bonanza* on television. When he stood in the door, the men and even some of the women stopped to stare at him. Albert was sitting in the corner reading the newspaper. When he saw Frank, he came shuffling up smiling at him, put his arm around him, turned and announced in a loud voice, "Friends, I want you to meet our new resident, Franklin Roberts."

Most of the men smiled, some just stared, and the curious women glared at him. Albert took his arm, led him around to each person and introduced him. Almost without fail, each person corrected Albert's formal name with their nickname. At the second pool table, he was introduced to a familiar face. "Of course you know Rudolph."

Ralph rolled his eyes exasperated. Frank smiled brightly and reached out his hand but his cranky neighbor turned to make a shot on the pool table. As Frank pulled back his hand, Ralph pulled the cue stick back and popped the cue ball sending it smashing into a cluster of balls near the opposite corner pocket. The balls scattered loudly, slamming into other balls on the table with only the cue ball finding the pocket. Ralph swore loudly and kicked the leg of the table.

The onlookers laughed and applauded. Ralph waved his hand in the air and nodded. "Yeah, yeah, fine."

Albert re-introduced him to Walter Montgomery, the large, heavyset man wearing an army vest, green khaki pants and brown boots that made him look like he was just back off a safari. Away from the breakfast table, "Monty" struck quite an imposing figure. The gentle giant fluttered his fingers while he gripped the cue stick with his thumb.

Frank judged him to be in his mid-seventies that would make him the young man in the room. Frank reached out to shake his huge hand. "Good to see you again."

Monty crushed his hand and shook it violently as he laughed with a wheeze. "Pa-pa-play pool, Frank?"

"Forty years ago, maybe."

Monty smiled and looked at Ralph. "Sa-Skill is not required, eh Ra-Ra-Ralph?"

Everyone chuckled at Ralph's expense as Monty placed the cue ball in line with the seven ball near the side pocket. He leaned over the table, placed his left fist on the table surface and laid the cue stick between his thumb and first knuckle, *like a kid or girl,* Frank thought to himself. Monty pulled back the cue and with a looping stroke chucked the cue ball into the bank missing the seven ball altogether.

Ralph snickered at his opponent as the onlookers cried "Awwwww." Monty good-naturedly chuckled at himself.

Albert led Frank to the television end of the room and started introducing him to three women sitting together on a couch in back. "Ladies, may I introduce to you Franklin Roberts."

The three women turned and glared at the new man. "Franklin, this is Gertrude, Judith, and Myrtle."

Gertrude giggled and added, "Albert is so formal. We go by Trudy, Judy, and Moody."

Judy chuckled but Moody was stoic. When Frank appeared to notice the contradiction, Trudy explained, "We call Myrtle 'Moody' because she is SO NOT moody."

Trudy and Judy cackled at their little joke, but Myrtle turned her head and let out a contemptuous huff. Frank could see that these ladies were close, fun-loving friends. "Trudy, Judy, and ..." he paused and studied Myrtle for a moment, "... Moody? It is a pleasure to meet you."

Moody nodded and smirked; Trudy and Judy smiled brightly and fluttered their eyelashes. Albert attempted humor. "These beautiful ladies are our 'Golden Girls.'"

Frank remembered the old TV Series, but could not see the resemblance. "So which one is Betty White?"

Judy and Moody both pointed to the pudgy, round faced Trudy with the bubbling eyes. She looked nothing like Betty White. Judy explained, "Trudy is a little scatter-brained sometimes."

Trudy giggled and blushed. Frank could not remember the names of the other main characters, but did remember the funny little lady who was one of the character's mother. "What about the mother?"

Judy and Trudy looked at each other puzzled, Moody remembered. "Sophia."

Trudy's eyes lit up and she exclaimed, "Oh, yeah, Sophia."

Judy said, "We don't have a Sophia."

Moody changed the subject. "You're the new resident that was sitting with Mr. Cook when he ... kicked the bucket."

Trudy and Judy erupted into nervous chuckles and put their hands over their mouths as if embarrassed.

Frank raised his shoulders. "Yes, I'm afraid so." He tried to put on a solemn face. "Such a tragic affair."

Moody huffed again. "So, you didn't know him."

Even Albert chortled at her candor. Frank laughed and acknowledged, "I sort of got to witness his ..."

Moody finished his sentence for him. "Belligerence? Bullying? Pompousness?"

Frank tilted his head to one side and raised his shoulders as if to say, "Yeah, I guess so."

Between giddy chuckles, Trudy managed to ask, "Did you kill him?"

She and Judy laughed loudly at her audaciousness, Moody added commentary. "You'd be a hero if you did."

Frank blushed and held up his hands. "I'm afraid I'm not the hero."

He felt Albert grip his arm as he addressed the Golden Girls, "Thank you, ladies."

They moved to the front of the room where four ladies were huddled together in front of the television. Frank recognized the wild hair and eyes of the woman who had stopped by his room while he was waiting for TJ. The same lady Mr. Cook had insulted with the Lizzie Borden song. Albert made the introduction official. "Ladies, please meet Mr. Franklin Roberts, our newest resident."

Before Albert could continue, Lizzie interrupted. "Yeah, we've met."

Albert glanced at Frank curiously. "Oh. Have you met ..."

Before he could introduce the other ladies, one jumped up, offered her hand and snapped, "Lucy."

She turned to the other two ladies. "That's Mary and Ruth."

Frank nodded. "Pleased to meet you."

The two women stared at him with stern, almost frightened looks. He found the ladies creepy and felt very uneasy. "Anything interesting on television?"

Mary and Ruth glanced at the television as if surprised by it. Lucy glanced at Lizzie as if seeking guidance. Lizzie smiled wryly at him, *Bonanza.*

Albert rescued him. "Well, we should let you get back to your program. Good day, ladies."

As they walked away, Frank thought he could feel their stares boring into the back of his neck.

Trudy and Judy fluttered their fingers at him as they went by. He noticed that Moody ignored him.

"You're up, Roberts!" someone yelled from the pool tables.

Chapter Twenty-Five

1:05 P.M. The Coroner's Report

W HEN THE SHERIFF AND his two deputies pulled up in front of the El Paso County Coroner's Office, they were surprised to see White Feather sitting on the curb in front of the door.

Buster spotted him first. "Well, looka there, our old friend, White Feather."

Morrison jerked his head around as Calhoun commented, "Still thinks it's a soup kitchen." He was referring to a previous homicide in which White Feather had sat in on the autopsy. The coroner and medical examiner, who had not met Morrison yet, assumed White Feather was the new deputy from Wet Mountain County. When they learned the truth, Calhoun had joked that White Feather must have been a vagrant looking for the soup kitchen.

The sheriff chuckled appeasingly. They bailed out of the sheriff's SUV and headed for the front door. White Feather stood and the sheriff greeted him. "Afternoon, White Feather. You're a long way from home."

White Feather shrugged and opened the door for his old friends. After signing in, their boots clattered loudly on the tile floor as they headed to the examining room where the coroner and medical examiner were waiting. They were shocked to see the Indian. It had only been a month or so since White Feather had joined them for that other autopsy. The sheriff had given the coroner and medical examiner a hard time when later they actually met Morrison.

The sheriff introduced them to the mysterious stranger. "John, Dr. Morgan, you remember White Feather I presume."

Their faces betrayed their embarrassment as they awkwardly nodded to White Feather. The Indian remained quiet and aloof.

The door creaked and drew their attention to the entry of CBI Agent Miles Blakeley. The stern man nodded and found a spot next to the sheriff. When he spotted White Feather, he frowned and protested, "Who the hell are you?"

Sheriff Bailey introduced him. "Miles, this is our friend White Feather. He is acting as a consultant for us today."

The contrary agent huffed. "Consultant? You're kidding, right?"

Bailey tried to deflect the agent. "Dr. Morgan was ..."

"You don't need a consultant, Bailey. This is official business. No place for friends and family."

All eyes focused on the sheriff who seemed unperturbed by the sarcastic agent. "You were saying Dr. Morgan."

All eyes turned to Dr. Morgan who also seemed eager to get on with it. "It was strychnine alright. We found a lethal amount in his system. It was definitely the cause of death."

The medical examiner waited for the information to sink in before adding, "We did not find the other toxins you would expect in rat poison."

Morrison challenged him. "So, it wasn't the rat poison?"

Dr. Morgan shrugged. "I would have to say that I doubt it. Can't say, though, for sure what it was. He had the oddest collection of herbs and concoctions I've ever encountered in his system."

Bailey tried to clarify. "So, you don't know what introduced the poison into his system?"

The medical examiner held out his hands. "It's a mystery, Sheriff."

Morrison inquired, "Did you bring over the toxicology report?"

Dr. Morgan shook his head. "Wasn't ready. They said they would send it over later."

Sheriff Bailey glanced at his deputies, nodded, and challenged the examiners. "Anything else?"

The examiners shrugged. Morrison was persistent. "Will the toxicology report give us the delivery agent?"

Dr. Morgan answered, "No way to tell for sure. Maybe."

Dr. Morgan examined their Native American friend. "So, White Feather working for you now, Sheriff?"

Bailey chuckled. "Let's just say he's working WITH us. White Feather was very helpful with the Ludwig murders. Nothing official, but I like to hear his opinion. As a man of medicine, I feel he could be very helpful with this case."

Dr. Morgan did not seem impressed. White Feather was stoic and kept his eyes closed as if unaware anyone was talking about him. Morrison chuckled at the dynamics of the personalities. White Feather would never have been allowed to join an investigation with the Denver P. D.

But, in the remote county of Wet Mountain Valley, pretenses were dropped and people seemed to accept each other more readily.

Smiles was not from a rural area. "That's a bunch of baloney and you know it."

Chapter Twenty-Six
6:05 P.M. The Dinner Club

WHEN FRANK ENTERED THE dining room, he was happy to find his new friends sitting together at the same table. He strolled over to the food cart, picked out his dinner tray and then went to the coffee bar to fill a glass with milk. Birdie walked through the double doors from the kitchen and stood fanning herself with a dish rag. When she noticed Frank, her eyes sparkled and she waddled over to him. "Mr. Roberts! Finding everything OK?"

She glanced at his glass. "Oh, honey, let me get you some fresh milk. I'll bet you like it cold."

Frank handed her his glass and beamed. "Oh, that would be wonderful. Thank you."

As she turned, she retorted, "No problem. A growing boy needs his milk."

She laughed heartily as she disappeared into the kitchen. Frank took his tray over to his friends' table where Albert smiled and waved him to an empty chair. As he sat, Albert remarked, "We reserved that chair for our pool shark."

Frank blushed and nodded to Monty, Ralph, and White Feather. Monty smiled brightly with raised eyebrows; Ralph ignored him. White Feather nodded impassively. Albert caught him up. "We were just discussing the curious death of the infamous Mr. Cook. White Feather was telling us that the coroner has officially pronounced Benjamin's death a homicide resulting from a lethal dose of strychnine poisoning."

Despite a mouthful of food, Ralph glanced at White Feather and jumped in, "Where'd you hear that?"

The old Cherokee wizard shrugged. "From the medical examiner."

Monty giggled and Ralph persisted, "From the medical examiner?"

White Feather reluctantly explained, "The sheriff is an old friend."

Albert inquired, "Does the sheriff have any suspects?"

White Feather slurped soup straight from the bowl, wiped his chin with the back of his hand and answered, "He didn't say."

White Feather added between slurps, "Everyone is a suspect."

Ralph frowned, but Albert seemed unsurprised as he resumed eating. Monty gasped and glanced around to check his friends for their reaction to such an outrageous comment.

Ralph opened up his hands. "Of course. We all hated the guy and anyone of us could've slipped poison into his drink or plate."

With wide eyes, Monty surmised, "They'll want to question all of us again."

Albert confirmed, "I'm sure they will."

Birdie sashayed up to the table with a big glass of milk. "My Lord! Now here's trouble if I ever seed it."

She laughed as she set the glass in front of Frank. Frank thanked her as the image of her little spat with Benny flashed into his head. He looked her over trying to decide if she looked like someone who could dump poison into someone's food ... or drink? He looked warily at his milk.

She wiped her hand on her apron and turned serious. "Sheriff said we can remove the yellow tape tomorrow, maybe. Doubt if anybody's gonna wanna sit there though."

Albert looked up. "Oh, I don't know, we might. As Benjamin would say, 'it has a nice view.'"

Birdie waved her hand in disgust. "Please don't mention that man to me. Lordy!"

She turned and waddled to the next table to visit. Monty raised his eyebrows and frowned at Albert as if appalled by his suggestion. Ralph pointed his fork at Monty's new potatoes. "You gonna eat all of those?"

Monty scowled at him and Ralph retreated. White Feather slid his tray over and Ralph saluted him with his fork before spearing several potatoes and transferring them to his plate.

Albert re-opened the subject of Cook's death. "Walter, when the deputy returns to question you, will you be able to clear yourself?"

Monty stuttered under his breath as he explored the space in front of him for answers. Ralph stopped to study his friend; White Feather set down his bowl; Frank took a drink of his milk but kept his eyes on Monty. Albert decided to help his flustered friend. "Well, you have motive, as all of us have. So, they must establish opportunity. Can you remember where you were Sunday? Can you prove where you were that day?"

Monty began to gasp and look about nervously. Albert tried to calm him. "You don't have to respond, Walter, we are your friends. But, we all should spend time reviewing our whereabouts and actions on that day."

White Feather weighed in. "Strychnine can take up to two hours and as little as ten minutes to take effect."

As Ralph munched on new potatoes, he asked, "What time did the bum die?"

Albert responded, "Around 12:45."

Ralph summarized, "So, we need to account for our whereabouts and actions from 10:45 to 12:35."

Albert corrected. "That is the window for ingestion. Unfortunately, we don't know when the poison was administered."

Ralph protested, "Speak English."

Frank gave his version. "Someone could have poisoned his food hours before he actually ate it."

Ralph's eyes reflected his eureka moment. Albert emphasized the point. "So, I suggest we each need to prepare for the sheriff's questions."

White Feather made a bold proposal. "Unless WE solve it."

Albert appeared to be confused, Monty's eyes lit up, and Frank smiled wryly. White Feather expanded on his idea. "We solve the crime; they go away."

Ralph stared at Monty and pointed out, "Unless one of US did it!"

Chapter Twenty-Seven

6:45 P.M. Ralph's Granddaughter

As the five old friends exited the dining room, Frank was the first to notice the female sheriff's deputy walking through the door from reception. She was stocky, average height, with a rugged face. Her nose was big and broad, her lips puffy and her mouth too wide. She was not ugly, but definitely not pretty and the scowl on her face reminded him of someone.

When she spotted the old men, she raised her hand and shouted, "Grampa!"

Ralph halted and looked up to see her. Without comment or visible reaction, he headed in her direction. Albert explained, "Ralph's granddaughter, Sydney Jacobs. She's a Wet Mountain County deputy."

Frank smiled. Now he recognized that scowl; it was the scowl of Ralph Jacobs. Frank watched the grumpy couple engage. There was no hugging and no smiles, just short back-and-forths. They turned and disappeared into the reception area.

"How have you been, Grampa?"

Ralph found a comfortable couch by a window across the room from Naomi, the receptionist. As he sat, he grumbled, "Terrific."

"You look good."

Ralph glared at his lying granddaughter. "Good compared to what? Your dog?"

Sydney chuckled, and replied softly, "No, not that good."

Ralph snorted trying to restrain a chuckle. She knew he loved her and appreciated her visits although he would never admit it. They sat in awkward silence for a moment until Ralph inquired, "You in on the investigation?"

Sydney looked at him with a blank stare and then remembered. "Oh, the Cook poisoning." She shifted and stared across the room. "No. The new guy's heading up that one. Did you see it go down?"

Ralph chuckled. "Hell, I was sittin' next to the bum."

"At his table?"

"Oh, no, not at his table. I hated him. But so did everybody else, I guess."

"You know who did it?"

Ralph shook his head. "No clue. Just wish I'd thought of it."

Sydney's scowl transformed into a cute smile, "Graaaampa, don't let anyone hear you say that."

Ralph stuck out his chin. "Why not? It's the truth."

Sydney's smile faded. She decided to change the subject. "Heard from Daddy. He's still in San Diego."

"What's he doin' there?"

Sydney shrugged. "It's that Fat Leonard scandal thing."

Ralph shook his head. "Can't even eat too much without JAG investigating you?"

Sydney laughed. "Bribery, Grampa. Fat Leonard is the guy that owns the company that was extorting information on government contracts."

Ralph persisted, "How you know so much? Ain't Jarod's investigations top secret?"

Sydney huffed, "It was in the news."

They returned to silence. Ralph and her father had not been on good terms since her Grampa and Grammy divorced. Her grandmother's clingy, needy personality had made it impossible for her father, Jarod, to remain neutral and the tension between him and Grampa was hard on Sydney.

Her grandmother had somehow managed to get Ralph's construction firm in the divorce settlement that had left him broken and bankrupt. Sydney was only eight when the divorce took place. She did not know all of the facts. All she knew was that her Grammy Maggie was an alcoholic and had moved back to Australia after the divorce.

She always dreaded visits to Grampa and Grammy's. Ralph was naturally a grumpy man, but around Grammy he was impossible. Grammy demanded the center of attention. She was always holding a wine glass and, as her father described it, "performing for her audience."

Sydney's mother was usually the target and hated the visits as much as Sydney. As a result, they limited their visits to Thanksgiving or Christmas each year.

After the divorce, Sydney had learned a new side of her grampa. Without the embarrassment and harassment of Grammy, he was not a bad guy. He was grumpy but good-hearted she had found, and they had become very close.

For as long as Sydney could remember, her father had traveled. His job as a Navy JAG investigator had required him to go on-site to investigate naval crimes. For years, she and her mother had accompanied him. But when her mother's mother fell ill, they had moved to Rockcliffe to take care of her. Sydney had enjoyed living in one spot, going to school and having long-term friends. So, she was delighted when after her grandmother died, they had remained in Rockcliffe.

After Ralph's bankruptcy, Jarod and Sydney insisted Ralph move to Rockcliffe so they could keep an eye on him. For a time, he worked on small construction projects for hire. But his health prevented him from working for very long. Her mother's association with the local Methodist church had enabled them to get Ralph accepted at St. Jude.

Her mother never really warmed to Ralph, but helped him in every way she could. Sydney knew Ralph well enough to know that he liked her mother, but his pride would never allow him to show any hint of affection.

Ralph startled her out of her distant thoughts. "Ever hear anything on the hag?"

Sydney's heart panged, not because of her Grampa's hateful description of her Grammy. She was an old hag and Sydney hated her, but it hurt because she knew how much Grammy had hurt Grampa and she was sad that he stooped to her level when he called her a hag.

Sydney took a deep breath and shared, "Daddy said she's in an institution. She thinks she's just in there for rehab, but Daddy says it's permanent."

Ralph spit out the words, "She's crazy as a loon."

Sydney could tell from his words and the way he expressed them that Ralph still felt a lot of hate and resentment. But, in a strange way, she thought she could detect the feelings of a man who felt deceived and hurt. He had probably loved her more than he ever showed or would admit. Sydney's father had once told her that although his mother had always been flamboyant and outgoing, she had not always been so self-absorbed and hateful. He blamed the alcohol. Sydney knew that he had fond memories from his childhood.

He had once told her that Grammy had always wanted to be an actress, but with Ralph's job, that was never going to be. So, she sort of saw parties and get-togethers as opportunities to be on stage.

Sydney felt that her father was rationalizing. Ralph's construction firm was in Long Beach, California, hardly an hour from Hollywood. Raising her father was more likely Grammy Maggie's roadblock to stardom.

"We oughta go into town to eat sometime."

"Costs too much."

Sydney started to explain that she could afford it and then realized that Ralph would never allow a girl to pay for his meal. She offered an alternative, "Maybe you could come over and I'll cook something."

Ralph was quiet and just stared straight ahead. She studied his blank expression. Not speaking was her grampa's way of telling her that he loved her but did not want to hang out with her. He was right. They did not really have much to talk about when they were alone. And her grampa was set in his ways and comfortable at St. Jude. The world away from St. Jude was of no interest to him anymore.

Chapter Twenty-Eight

11:00 P.M. The Journal/
The Phone Call

SAMANTHA MORRISON FELT THE tension on the spring tighten and removed the key from the old German clock above the mantel. She stepped down off the hearth in front of the fireplace and strolled across the shadowy room to check the sliding door. It was locked. She strode past the small, galley-style kitchen and through the living room to check the front door.

The kids were asleep, the house secure, now it was her time. As she stepped back into the light of the kitchen, she could hear the tea kettle revving up to whistle. She turned off the burner, removed it just in time and poured it over the tea bag hanging in her china cup. She set the kettle on a dormant burner and picked up her tea cup.

She flipped off the light in the kitchen and paused to let her eyes adjust. Guided only by the night light glowing in the hallway, she headed for her bedroom at the end of the long hall. The old German clock started striking in cadence with her steps, eleven bells and eleven steps to her bedroom.

She switched on the lamp by her poster bed, took a sip of the hot tea, set down her tea cup on a coaster, opened the drawer and removed her private journal.

Once settled in her bed, she began to write:

Dear Journal,

   He didn't call tonight. I'm glad. I was ready to give him a piece of my mind. But, I have no right to complain. We're divorced. I have no claims on his private life. I would have made a fool out of myself.

   Still, it hurts. I guess I never thought about him dating. I never thought about him getting over me and moving on. And when he came to Rockcliffe and got back in touch with us, well, I had hoped for ... well, I don't know what I hoped for.

Samantha put down the pen and picked up her tea cup. As she sipped the tepid brew, she decided that was "enough said."

Across town, Samantha's ex-husband, Sam Morrison, lay in bed staring at the darkness above him. He glanced over at the night table, it was eleven ten. He took a deep breath, or more like a sigh of relief, because it was definitely too late to call Samantha now.

He had spent all evening taking turns worrying about a homicide and worrying about his relationship with Samantha and the kids. He had picked up the phone and set it back down dozens of times. She had been very understanding last evening when he had called after that exhausting day at St. Jude investigating the Cook homicide.

He had told her he would call and reschedule. And although he had intended to call her that evening, in the end, he had rationalized that since she knew he was busy with the case, she would also understand when he did not call back right away. She knew that he had always been dedicated to his work.

Of course, that was a bad argument. He had always been too dedicated. That was the reason for their divorce. That was the reason she moved so far from Denver, so far away from him.

If he had any chance of rebuilding their relationship, he would need to show her that he had changed; that she and the kids were number one in his life now.

It would be after this mental argument with himself that he would pick up the phone. Then visions of Darla's unwelcome visit would flash in his head and what Samantha would most likely conclude if she got wind of the visit. That would prompt him to slam down the phone before it could ring.

So, in the end, he had not made the call.

Tuesday

Chapter Twenty-Nine

6:35 A.M. Plan Your Work, Work Your Plan

IT WAS THE BEGINNING of fall and the autumn of life for the residents of St. Jude Methodist Retirement Center. The old failed hospital converted into a retirement home lay hidden amid a small, remote, dense forest. The qualification for residency was destitution—St. Jude was a home for lost causes.

Eighty-seven-year-old resident Franklin Damon Roberts did not think of himself as a lost cause! Not that day, anyway.

Frank was awake very early. He lay staring up at the ceiling lamenting the fact that he had no plans for the day. Before his homeless years, he had been a planner. He liked to plan his work and work his plan. He liked to make checklists and felt good checking off each item as it was completed. Frank tried to remember the last time he had made a checklist, but it had been too many years.

Motivated, he threw the covers off and rolled out of bed. He rushed to the chest of drawers and carefully selected his wardrobe for the day. Today he wanted to look like a million dollars! Today was a new day and he was anxious to make it the start of a new life as well.

After dressing, Frank searched the room for pen and paper, but without success. Undeterred, he rushed out of his room and headed for the administrative offices of the home. Only the elevators with red doors went to the top floor of the facility where the administrative offices resided. Frank happily pushed the "up arrow" next to the red doors.

As he waited for the elevator, he caught a glimpse of a nurse's uniform approaching. Nurse Nujent reached out to push the "up arrow" on the red door but stopped short when she realized the arrow had already been pushed. Recognizing Frank, she glared at him and demanded, "Mr. Roberts! What are you doing? Where are you going?"

"Good morning, Mrs. Nujent. I'm going up to admin' to get a pen and paper. I realized that I don't have any in my room, and I've decided that I want to make a list of 'Things to Do' today!"

Nurse Nujent frowned. "Residents aren't allowed to use the red doors, Mr. Roberts! Besides, pens are dangerous. Now run along, it's about time for breakfast."

"Dangerous? How is a pen dangerous?"

"Now don't be difficult, Mr. Roberts. Come on, I'll walk you to the dining room."

As the nurse reached for Frank's arm, he pulled away. The elevator doors opened. Frank looked at the empty elevator, then at the fussy nurse. Nurse Nujent's brow furrowed. She looked at Frank curiously and then at the elevator ... then aimed a stern, condescending look at Frank. "Mr. Roberts?"

Frank's pulse quickened; he stared at the elevator; he could feel it beckoning, drawing him in.

Nujent's voice squeaked slightly. "OK, Mr. Roberts. Come on, let's go!"

The elevator doors closed. The pesky nurse reached again for Frank's arm. Frank put his palms up and sidled by the nurse. "That's OK, I know the way to the dining room."

"You're up early, Frank."

Frank looked up to find the home's jovial head cook. The plump, black woman stood over him with her fists resting on her ample hips. Frank shrugged as he stirred the scrambled eggs with his fork. "Hi, Birdie."

"Your buddies won't be down for another hour, you know."

Frank shrugged.

Birdie examined his plate. "Aren't you hungry?"

She pulled back a chair and plopped down beside him. "So, what is it Frank?"

"Oh, nothing, Birdie. I guess I'm just not hungry."

"Ooo-Kaaay!" The no-nonsense woman gave Frank a condescending look.

Frank chuckled. He knew that he would not win this one. "It's that dang Nurse Nujent."

Birdie reared back omnisciently nodding her head and folded her arms. "Her again."

Frank looked confused. "Again?"

"That woman is always upsetting some nice resident and spoiling their lovely appetites. What'd she do this time?"

"I needed a pen and paper. Well, according to Nurse Nujent, pens are dangerous."

Birdie rocked back in an uproarious cackle slapping her knees with her hands. Then she leaned forward, placed her fleshy elbows on the table and put on her most serious face. She smiled with a twinkle in her eye and then glanced around guiltily as if checking to make sure no one was watching. Stealthily, she pulled a pencil out of her apron pocket, folded a napkin over it and slid them across the table to Frank.

Frank smiled and pushed it back. "Thanks, anyway, Birdie, but I don't need it anymore."

Birdie turned her head and looked at Frank sideways. She studied him for a moment, long enough to make Frank uneasy. "You need it, Frank."

Frank looked at the determined woman. "I do?"

"How can you write me a love note if you don't have a pencil and paper?"

The two enjoyed an uplifting laugh.

Frank strode proudly out of the dining room with Birdie's gift boldly riding behind his right ear hoping he would run into Nurse Nujent. As he turned down the corridor toward the elevator, instead of nurse Nujent, the administrator of the home suddenly appeared, shrieked, folded her arms across her body, and stopped just short of running into the pen rebel.

Frank put up his hands and instinctively muttered, "Scuse me, Mrs. Barkley."

As quickly as she had put up her defenses, Mrs. Barkley recovered and dipped her head at the startled man. "Good morning, Mr. Roberts." She raised her chin and charged on down the hallway.

Frank glanced back at the confident lady and breathed a sigh of relief. When he turned back to continue his own journey, he found himself face-to-face with a frowning Nurse Nujent. The unpleasant woman plucked Frank's pencil from behind his ear, held it up with both hands in front of his nose, and snapped it in two!

Frank looked into the smug woman's eyes and heard himself say, "Will you be needing both of those, Nurse Nujent?"

The disgusted nurse stormed off in a huff sucking the exuberance that Frank had just regained out of him again.

Chapter Thirty

7:45 A.M. Frank Meets
with White Feather

F‌RANK PACED IN HIS room trembling with rage and humiliation. In his mind, he imagined all manner of retaliation against his now hated enemy, Nurse Nujent. He imagined stabbing the horrified woman with a Bic pen! "Pens are dangerous? I'll show you dangerous!"

Then he felt a little pang of guilt and embarrassment. He tried to formulate clever put-downs and retorts. But nothing pithy came to mind. Soon, the whole episode just left him tired and depressed. He plopped down in his tattered old recliner and took a deep breath to try to regain his calm.

After a few moments, he realized that he had to get out—completely out of the St. Jude Prison. He appreciated what Judy had done for him, but, after living homeless for five years, maybe it was too late for him to go back. Maybe he was no longer cut out for civilization. He dragged himself up, pulled a jacket out of the chest of drawers, and stared at the gym bag trying to decide if he should pack all of his things. It seemed like a lot of trouble. Maybe he would reconnoiter today so he could plan a clean getaway for tomorrow. He slipped on the jacket and headed for downstairs.

The humiliated old man stepped through the back door into the dreary, overcast morning. The humidity made the air feel dank and chilled. Frank pulled his jacket collar up and shuffled across the lawn to a narrow strip of trees with dense vegetation underneath. A narrow path led him through the wind break to the small lake only about fifty yards beyond. A lonely, gnarled tree grew stubbornly beside the lake.

He shivered slightly and took in a chilling breath of the crisp morning air. The feeling took him back to his homeless years when there were days when there was no hope of relief from the bitter cold. How quickly he had become spoiled by the warmth and shelter of St. Jude.

A brown "inhabited" bundle sat on a park bench facing the gnarly tree and the lake. As Frank approached, he could not make out who the person in the bundle might be since the blanket was pulled up over the head like a hood. The ground was crumpled and uneven around the gnarly tree's roots and Frank found it difficult to walk. Despite several stumbles accompanied by angry epithets, the bundle did not turn around or appear to notice his clumsy approach.

Frank reached out and gripped the back of the bench causing it to rock back, but still the bench resident remained aloof. "May I join you?" Frank blurted out as he fell onto the bench.

Whatever was wrapped in the bulky, brown blanket remained rigid and still. Frank could not see the face of the disinterested occupant for the hood covering its head. He gingerly leaned forward to peek inside the hood and was startled by the grotesque face in the blanket!

Round, white eyes that appeared to almost be glowing, stared at the gnarled tree in front of the bench. Bluish, thin skin sagged almost transparently on the face of the skull. Gray, natty hair was poking out from under the hood like a spray of grass. A white owl's feather dangled to one side tipping off Frank that behind the blanket was the home's token Indian, the weird old shaman, White Feather.

Frank sat back and stared at the deformed tree wondering what about it had fixed the Indian's attention. Frank was startled by a raspy, whisper from the blanket, "What do you make of this tree?"

Frank looked at the crooked old tree. Thick roots jutted out and intertwined as they extended above and under the ground, reaching out toward the bench. The trunk appeared to be three trees that had fought each other for space and grown together in the battle. "Looks like three or more trees sprouted from the same spot, maybe."

"Hmmph!" The old Indian commented.

After a long pause, Frank challenged, "What do you make of it?"

The Indian was silent. He appeared in no hurry to respond. Finally, a husky, whispering, question, "Three different trees? ... Or the same tree repeated?"

Frank contemplated the curious new challenge and wondered, *Do Indians work at being mysterious or is it in their genes?* "I'd say three different trees."

"Hmmph."

The following silence prompted Frank to revisit the question. To his surprise, he discovered that the three trees were, in fact, identical in shape. Every branch and every bend and twist in the trunks was mirrored in the next tree. But, curiously, they were slightly different sizes. The tree to the left was larger than the tree next to it to the right which was larger than the tree to its right.

White Feather seemed to change the subject, "Man with circular calendar."

Frank was taken aback. Then he remembered that he had drawn a circle on the back of the calendar TJ had given him and written the months counter-clockwise around the circle. It was the way he had always visualized the year and was easier for him to reference than the traditional calendar. "Yeah, that would be me."

"You see time."

Frank swiveled around on the bench. "I don't know. I don't see a clock anywhere and I hocked my watch five years ago."

The bulging bundle was shaking with laughter. "Don't care what time it is."

Frank shook his head but did not respond, prompting the old man to continue, "You have something rare. You SEE time."

Frank was confused and feeling uncomfortable. This was starting to feel like one of those annoying conversations with a drunk "know-it-all" in a bar that is full of science fiction or political conspiracies.

The Indian persisted, waving his hand in a wide, horizontal circle. "You see time as a huge circle. Your position on the circle depends upon the time of the year.

The days and months progress counter-clockwise around the circle."

Frank realized that was exactly how he pictured the year. But, he had never thought anything of it and presumed that everyone pictured the year in his own way. "How do you picture it?"

The Indian chuckled again. "I don't see anything. Most people don't. But, you are connected to time. You can see it."

"I don't ACTUALLY SEE it. I just have my own way of visualizing it."

"Hummph."

Frank searched for a way to excuse himself from this weird conversation, but the Indian continued, "Explain why others like you describe the year EXACTLY the same way."

Frank frowned as he reluctantly responded, "Like me?"

"Others that can see time."

Frank shifted on the bench. "Oh, I don't suppose that my method of visualizing the year is all that unique. It's just a circle."

"Ever seen it shown that way?"

Frank thought about it and had to admit, "I don't think so—EXACTLY. But I think I've seen it portrayed as a circle before."

"With months COUNTER-CLOCKWISE?"

Frank realized that he had never seen anything portrayed counter-clockwise. He remained quiet, waiting, but White Feather remained quiet also.

The chilling breeze let up as if Nature held her breath waiting for the stalemate to end. But, she would only hold her breath for so long. Frank could feel the mist thickening and then the breeze pick up again. He was starting to shiver and longed to return to the warmth of the building, but he did not want to be rude. As if sensing his discomfort, the shivering old Indian leaned forward and eased off the bench onto his feet. "Time for breakfast."

Chapter Thirty-One
8:05 A.M. Breakfast

W<small>HITE</small> F<small>EATHER AND</small> F<small>RANK</small> found Albert and Monty dining quietly at the same table—not Benny's table. The buffet awaited, but Frank was hesitant. "I don't know if I should go through again, I was here earlier."

Without looking at him, White Feather resolved the issue. "You hungry?"

Frank rubbed his stomach. "Yeah, actually."

"We are allowed unlimited seconds."

With that, White Feather headed for the plates. Frank smiled. "Yeah, I guess that's right," and followed him.

Birdie walked out of the kitchen and spotted him. "Hi, Frank. Bring me a love letter?"

Frank smiled brightly. "I'm still working on it. Has to be just right for someone special as you."

She laughed happily, as she wiped her hands on her apron and then pointed a finger at him. "You like milk with your meal, I'll get it."

Frank felt embarrassed. "If it's not too much trouble."

When he turned back to catch up with White Feather, he bumped into Ralph holding his plate piled high in one hand and a cup of steaming coffee in the other. The startled grump successfully juggled the plate and cup. "Crap."

"Oh, sorry, Ralph."

Ralph raised his eyebrows and headed for the tables. Frank found his neighbor's saunter comical in his huge red canvas shoes, his wild, Hawaiian-style pullover shirt, and purple shorts exposing his thin, hairy legs. In his mind, Frank could hear flop, flop, flop as Ralph plodded to the table like a snorkeler wearing flippers on his feet.

After they filled their plates, White Feather and Frank approached the table where Monty greeted them enthusiastically and Albert smiled and waved to chairs for them to sit. Frank's heart warmed as he gratefully took his seat. White Feather sat down without comment or notice.

Albert waited until everyone was settled and then opened with, "So, is everyone ready for questioning?"

Monty gasped but White Feather and Ralph appeared to ignore him. Frank answered, "I suppose I am. I don't think I have a motive, so I doubt if I'm a suspect."

Monty fidgeted with his silverware and nodded nervously. Ralph scooped up a spoonful of scrambled eggs and stuffed it into his mouth while White Feather picked up a slice of pineapple and started gnawing on it. Albert responded, "I expect that is true, Franklin."

He took a bite of sausage and stared at Ralph. The wrinkled face of the grumpy man scowled back. "What're you lookin' at?"

Albert smiled and asked, "Have you solved the crime yet, Rudolph?"

Ralph grumbled as he continued to chew his food. Albert continued, "Then have you figured out what you are going to tell the sheriff when he questions you?"

Ralph chewed for a moment more, swallowed, then said, "Everbody knows you did it."

White Feather and Monty almost choked on their food. Albert shook his head. "Maybe that will work for you, Rudolph."

Monty was eager to share his discovery. "I've learned something interesting."

Ralph and White Feather ignored him, but Albert smiled and asked, "What did you learn, Walter?"

Monty glanced around at the other tables and then whispered, "Lizzie visited the kitchen that day."

Ralph stopped eating and looked at Monty. Albert followed up with, "How did you discover that, Walter?"

Monty beamed a great prideful smile. "I overheard her tell Ruth that Birdie had told her to get out of her kitchen and she had told Birdie she could go into the kitchen anytime she wanted."

Albert nodded to Monty. "Very good, Walter. Did she say when that happened?"

Monty's bright smile faded. Ralph huffed and returned to his food. Albert did not give up on him. "When did you hear the conversation?"

Monty raised his eyebrows tentatively. "Last night."

Birdie arrived with Frank's milk. "A lot of whispering goin' on over here."

Albert blotted his lips with his napkin. "We hear that Elizabeth may have been in the kitchen the day of Benjamin's demise?"

White Feather cleared his throat. Albert gasped. "Oh, I'm sorry White Feather, I forgot about the spirit thing."

White Feather shrugged. "It's not me you should apologize to."

Birdie frowned at the two men. Albert explained, "White Feather has shared with us that after death, the soul begins a search for the ancestors. If you say his name, it calls him back from his journey."

Birdie shook her head and pointed to the floor. "Pshaw! That man's soul is headed down there if you ask me."

Ralph blurted out, spitting eggs, "That's what I said."

They all enjoyed a good laugh. Albert restated his question, "So, was Elizabeth in the kitchen that dreadful day?"

Birdie placed her fists on her hips. "Well, aren't we the little detectives this morning?"

Ralph exclaimed, "Was she or not?"

Birdie cackled and then raised her eyebrows. "Maybe."

Ralph cursed under his breath and gulped down a drink of his coffee. Birdie got serious. "I had forgotten about that, but she did come in to complain about us never having freshly squeezed orange juice for breakfast."

Albert inquired, "When was that?"

Birdie rolled her eyes up. "Would have been while we were preparing lunch."

Albert followed up with, "Could she have slipped something into ... someone's food?"

Birdie snorted and then thought about it. "I don't see how. How would she know which tray was Benny's?"

White Feather cleared his throat and whispered a prayer.

Monty chattered in the background, "Ooo ooo! Good point."

Frank had an idea. "Were the trays filled yet?"

Birdie pondered the question. "Well, some of 'em mighta' been."

Frank proposed, "Maybe Lizzie took him a tray?"

All eyes turned to Birdie. "Usually he got it on his way in, unless he saw someone he could boss around."

Albert persisted, saying, "How about that day?"

Birdie shook her head. "I don't really know. I was busy cooking so I don't know when ..." she glanced at White Feather, smirked and added, "SOMEONE came in."

Albert did not give up. "Did Elizabeth leave with a tray?"

Birdie's eyes rolled up again as she rubbed her chin with her fingers. "You know, I believe she may have."

Albert looked at White Feather and raised one eyebrow. Ralph, Monty and Frank waited for a response from the old shaman. White Feather looked across the room at Lizzie and her friends entering the dining room.

Ralph stuffed another spoonful of eggs into his mouth and then commented as he chewed, "Here she comes. Why don't you ask her, Stein?"

Albert was undeterred. "Perhaps that is a job more suitable for a blunt man?"

Ralph frowned. "Me?"

All eyes trained on him waiting for a response. Without a pause, Ralph hollered, "Lizzie," and waved her over to the table.

The woman with wild, white hair scowled at him as she approached the table. "Wha'dya want, Jacobs?"

Ralph looked down at his plate and scooped up hash browns. "Stein has something to ask you."

Lizzie glared at Albert and waited. Albert scowled at Ralph and then smiled at the impatient woman. "Ralph is too shy to ask, Elizabeth, but I think he wants to know if you took a tray to Benjamin Sunday at lunch?"

"Why?" she asked with a scowl on her face.

Without blinking an eye, Albert explained, "I think he is jealous."

Ralph choked, White Feather, Birdie and Frank busted out laughing; Monty was confused. Lizzie huffed skeptically and glared at Ralph. "Tell him I hope he chokes to death."

Monty reached over to slap the choking man on the back just as he placed his coffee cup to his lips causing him to slam into it, spilling coffee on his prized Hawaiian shirt. Even Lizzie could not help laughing at the humiliated man.

Albert returned to the point. "Someone says they saw you taking a tray from the kitchen that day. Was it for you or for ..." He avoided speaking the dead man's name.

Lizzie turned to Albert and whispered, "The person you need to talk to is Katie Mae." The mysterious woman raised her eyebrows and then shuffled off to the buffet.

Albert turned to look at the attractive black woman sitting with Judy, Trudy, and Moody. Frank and Monty followed Albert's eyes and spotted the woman in her early sixties sitting quietly with the chattering "Golden Girls." Her head rested on her propped up hand and she looked sad and distant. Birdie was confused, "Katie Mae?"

Ralph quipped as he was wiping off his shirt, "Everyone who believes Katie Mae is the killer, raise his hand."

Monty beamed and started to raise his hand but paused when he saw that no one else's hand was in motion. Albert had an idea. "White Feather, do you think your friends at the sheriff's office could get access to the old institution files?"

Birdie's eyes grew large. "Mmm-mmmm. You boys are too much! You oughta call yourselves the Sleuthkateers."

She turned and as she walked away, muttered, "Mmm hmm. That's what I'm gonna call you, the Five Sleuthkateers," then she laughed loudly.

Chapter Thirty-Two

Reading, Pool, the Paper, and a Strange Request

As the "Five Sleuthkateers" rode up the elevator, Ralph goaded Monty into a rematch of pool. Frank was not offended that Ralph had not picked him. Monty was one of the few residents Ralph could depend upon to play as badly as him. So, not being challenged was a sideways compliment.

Albert followed his friends to the rec' room and found his favorite old Victorian chair to sit in and read the paper. Frank decided to spend the rest of his morning across the corridor in the parlor reading.

He found an interesting book called *Retirement Homes Are Murder*, by Mike Befeler. It was a humorous book about a man with no long-term memory trying to solve a murder in a retirement home. With a title like that, Frank could not resist.

No one could remember ever seeing White Feather in the rec' room, so no one missed him or wondered what he might be doing.

In town, Deputy Sam Morrison was late for work. He had spent the night tossing and turning and fretting over Darla's daring visit several evenings before. He could not help worrying about the consequences if word of the rogue waitress's visit got back to Samantha. He spent the night debating whether he should tell her himself before she found out. Otherwise, she was sure to conclude that he had canceled an evening with her and the kids so he could be with a local minx.

But when he rehearsed his confession, it always felt wrong. It might be presumptuous of him to think that he owed her any explanation. They were divorced. His life was his life; hers was hers. So, he had avoided calling her to reschedule until he could make a decision. Thus, the battle had raged in his mind long after he had gone to bed.

As Morrison opened the back door to the sheriff's office, he felt his stomach grumbling, craving strong, black, hot coffee. He rounded the corner and entered the open area where fellow deputies were engrossed in trading stories between day and night shifts. They ignored him as he dashed into the break room to satisfy his morning addiction.

His thoughts turned to the young girl they called "Gabby" in dispatch. He felt the bite of anxiety re-membering his awkward attempt to flirt with her the previous morning.

Uninterested in the macho bantering of the deputies, Morrison strolled by to catch a glimpse of Gabby. She was not at her desk, but as he moved closer, he could barely hear the muffled sound of her voice. She was standing behind the partition speaking to someone at the small glass window used by visitors.

He froze in place when she stepped back and walked to her desk to pick up the phone. As she lifted the phone to her ear, she noticed Morrison and put down the phone and waved him over.

"White Feather is here and wants to speak with someone."

Morrison smiled. He was curious what would bring the old shaman to the sheriff's office. He punched in the code to open the door to the reception area and stepped in. White Feather turned slowly and nodded. Morrison greeted him, "White Feather, What brings you to town?"

"A request."

Morrison raised his eyebrows. "OK, Come on back."

After declining coffee, White Feather followed Morrison to the small conference table in the open area. They drew the stares of the other deputies as Morrison offered the mysterious Indian a chair and then sat down adjacent to him. He took a careful sip of his steaming coffee, then looked at his colleagues causing them to scatter like a covey of quail.

He turned back to the old Indian. "A request?"

White Feather sat on the front edge of the chair with his hands gripping his knees. "Do you have access to the files of the old insane asylum?"

Morrison frowned as if asking "are you serious," then sat back and questioned, "Insane asylum?"

White Feather studied him for a moment and then explained, "St. Jude was an insane asylum many years ago."

Morrison's brow furrowed. "You don't say?"

White Feather added, "Elizabeth was a patient."

Now, he had the deputy's attention. "Elizabeth? Lizzie with the wild hair?"

White Feather chuckled and nodded.

"I don't know. I'd have to ask. What do you want to know?"

White Feather explained, "We want to see Elizabeth's records."

Morrison took another sip and then set down the mug and plucked a pencil from a round can in the center of the table and a small notepad. "Who is 'we'?"

White Feather did not blink. "Albert Stein and myself."

Morrison wrote Elizabeth Dawson on the notepad followed by White Feather and Albert Stein, circled White Feather and sat back. "Why do you want her records?"

White Feather clasped his hands. "Looking for the source of her devil spirit."

Morrison chuckled, but when White Feather remained stern, changed his demeanor. "Her devil spirit, eh?"

White Feather did not respond.

Morrison leaned forward and dropped the pencil back into the holder then sat back again. He pictured the crazy woman with wild hair. It might be interesting to look into her background. "You know where the records are kept?"

"Denver."

Morrison glanced at the sheriff's office, Sean was out. "I'll see what I can do."

White Feather nodded but remained seated. Morrison asked, "How'd you get here? You need a ride back?"

White Feather shook his head. "Rode in with library group."

Morrison smiled. "When does the bus pick you up?"

"Ten-thirty."

Morrison glanced at his watch. It was nine. "What you doin' 'til then?"

White Feather looked at the cork board, but did not answer. Morrison looked at the board. "You got any ideas on the murder?"

White Feather's expression grew very serious. "Those your suspects?"

Morrison looked back at the board. "So far. What do you think?"

White feather shook his head. Morrison tried to put himself into White Feather's head. He studied the board with pictures of the suspects across the top. "They all had access to poison. They all had reason to hate Mr. Cook."

The muscles in White Feather's temples rippled. "Do not speak the name of the dead."

Morrison was puzzled. White Feather explained, "His spirit is seeking his ancestors. Do not call him back."

Morrison nodded as he considered the old Indian's point. He found the notion charming, respectful, and elegant. "Forgive me." He rephrased his statement. "They had reason to hate the victim."

"Perhaps they possessed hatred, but the resolve?" White Feather raised his eyebrows to emphasize the wisdom of his words.

Morrison studied the list through this new filter. TJ was still a teenager, maybe twenty; a school girl whose thoughts were probably preoccupied with boys and school, not devious murder. Birdie was a caring, loving woman who looked at the residents as her children—a fussy hen looking after her chicks. Would she conspire to cull one of them for the benefit of the others? Probably not.

Morrison looked at Elizabeth Dawson's picture. "What about Lizzie?"

White Feather looked into Morrison's eyes. "Impulsive, not devious."

Morrison nodded. "I see what you mean. She might strangle him. She would be in his face, but not plot something behind his back."

But, Morrison was confused. "But, you still want to see her records?"

White Feather nodded. Morrison raised his eyebrows. "Mrs. Wilson, on the other hand ..."

White Feather squinted at Morrison and then looked back at the cork board. Morrison felt a little surge of pride. Had he impressed this wise Indian? He waited for White Feather's response.

The old wizard rubbed the back of his lips against his teeth. Morrison prompted him. "Getting his tea and then setting the glass just out of his reach shows a bit of deviousness."

White Feather corrected him. "Harmless spite."

Morrison persisted. "She's a strong woman; very protective of Mr. Wilson; no-nonsense type."

White Feather closed his eyes. "Hmmph."

Morrison was not sure whether White Feather was ceding the point or dismissing it altogether. He glanced back up at the board. "Nujent?"

White Feather smiled, or perhaps grimaced, but kept his eyes closed. Morrison smiled proudly. *He likes her for a suspect!* "Devious, cunning, strong ..."

White Feather slowly opened his eyes and stared at the floor. "Sad, lonely."

He turned his eyes to meet Morrison's. "No motive."

Morrison felt his face get warm. *No motive?* Morrison looked for a reason to contradict the wise man, but realized he might be right. "What's her story?"

White Feather shook his head thoughtfully. "Carries a dark secret, a heavy weight. Goes back many years. Searching for solace."

Morrison felt a new and deep sympathy for the nurse. White Feather had moved him. The old Cherokee had also thrown all of the suspects out of the window. Now, none of them seemed very likely.

Morrison cocked his head to one side. "If you don't suspect Lizzie, why do you want her file?"

White Feather gave him a look of disbelief. Morrison shifted in his chair. "Oh, yes, you want to find out where she got that devilish attitude."

White Feather did not answer. Morrison rubbed his nose and mouth. "We're driving out this afternoon to do some follow-up. I'll let you know if I have found out anything."

White Feather nodded, rose and shuffled off. Morrison drummed his fingers on the table and thought about the strange request. White Feather had piqued his curiosity. Now, he wanted to get a look at that file, too.

Chapter Thirty-Three

3:15 P.M. Follow Up Interviews

MORRISON ENTERED THE RECEPTION area of St. Jude Retirement Center and approached the attractive, professionally dressed receptionist sitting at the desk at the back of the room. "Hello, Mrs. Johnson," Morrison greeted.

Naomi stood and handed him a sheet of paper. "Here is the schedule for interviews the sheriff requested. I've got you in the north reception area."

Morrison accepted the list and thanked her. She led him down the first floor corridor to the other reception area in the northeast corner of the building. As they entered the room, Morrison spotted White Feather sitting cross-legged on the floor staring out the window. Morrison turned to Naomi. "Agent Blakeley is supposed to join me. Would you show him back when he comes in?"

Naomi rolled her eyes, nodded and left. Morrison approached White Feather. "Afternoon, White Feather."

The meditating wizard opened his eyes and nodded. White Feather held up his arms. Morrison helped the old man to his feet and escorted him to the couch. White Feather rubbed his thighs and muttered, "Just can't sit like that anymore."

Morrison shared a laugh with him as the old Indian dropped onto the couch and exhaled as if exhausted. Morrison pulled a chair up close and questioned, "Have anything for us?"

White Feather rubbed his legs again and began. "Elizabeth visited the kitchen Sunday; complained about the orange juice; may have left with a tray."

Morrison made a note and then studied the old man. "You think Elizabeth may have tampered with his, the victim's, tray?"

White Feather shrugged. "Elizabeth suggested we talk to Katie Mae."

"Katie Mae? What did she mean? Katie Mae took Cook a tray?"

White Feather cautioned, "Do not speak the name of the dead."

Morrison apologized. White Feather suggested, "Unlikely his lady friend poisoned him."

Morrison finished scribbling in his notebook. "Anything else?"

White Feather looked at Morrison and waited. Morrison looked up. "I requested the file on Elizabeth; may take several days; a lot of red tape."

Agent Blakeley entered the room. "File? What file?"

Morrison made another note, put up his hand to silence the agent, looked at White Feather and asked again, "Anything else?"

"Franklin Roberts has good eyes, a keen observer."

Blakeley protested. "He our first interview?"

Morrison assured White Feather. "We'll talk to him again," then he turned to the agent and said, "No, Elizabeth Dawson is first."

Blakeley glared at White Feather. "So, what's he doin' in here. I hope you're not thinking he's going to join us."

Chapter Thirty-Four

3:30 P.M. Follow Up with Lizzie

MORRISON AND BLAKELEY EXCHANGED strained cordialities and then sat quietly to wait for the first interviewee.

Diana Elizabeth Austin Dawson was late. Morrison listened intently for her footsteps. Subtle noises emanated from the walls as if ghosts were restless and whispering. Morrison shifted in his chair. All old buildings seemed to have their odd noises caused by the aging structures' creaking and shifting or the steam filling the vents or the water pipes clanking and rattling.

Morrison glanced at his watch, and shifted in his chair. Blakeley looked at his watch. "What time is the interview?"

Morrison grumbled, "Ten minutes ago."

Blakeley listened to his watch and then looked at it again. Morrison stood and walked to the doorway to look down the corridor at the elevator. As if prompted by his action, the bell on the elevator dinged and the doors slowly opened. A wispy figure with wild, white hair and a long, flowing white dress, or perhaps night gown, glided into the corridor and headed toward him. He recognized the spooky appearance of Lizzie. He turned and announced, "She's coming."

His comment startled Blakeley out of a dream and left him scrambling to reconnect with reality. Morrison turned to greet the scary lady, "Good afternoon, Mrs. Dawson."

Lizzie stopped, glared at him, and then at Blakeley. "Who are you?"

He snarled, "Agent Miles Blakeley with CBI."

Lizzie snarled back, "Takes two of you?"

Morrison motioned toward the couch. "Please be seated. We just have a few questions."

Lizzie turned and chose a high-backed chair in the corner of the room. Morrison and Blakeley exchanged glances and then Morrison dragged his chair over to her. Blakeley reluctantly followed with his chair. Lizzie started searching around her chair and then spit on the floor. Morrison stopped and studied the strange woman. He placed his chair and sat down. Blakeley studied her for a moment before joining Morrison. Morrison began his questions. "On the day of Mr. Cook's death, what time did you go to the dining room?"

Lizzie looked up at the ceiling. "I ain't got no watch."

Morrison studied her wrists and looked for a locket to confirm she was not wearing a time piece. "Was there anyone else in the dining room when you arrived?"

Lizzie took a deep, agonizing breath. "Cooks were there, nobody else."

Morrison made a note. "Are you usually the first one there?"

Lizzie folded her arms. "Nope."

Blakeley shifted impatiently in his chair. Morrison continued, "Why were you early that day?"

Lizzie breathed out in disgust. "They don't serve good orange juice. I wanted to discuss it with Birdie."

"Did you discuss it with Birdie?"

"Yep."

Morrison waited. Lizzie did not add anything so Morrison prompted her. "What did you do after that?"

Lizzie sniffed and recrossed her legs. "Grabbed a tray and went into the dining room to eat."

There was a curious creaking sound coming from behind the wall that adjoined the room to the south. Morrison and Blakeley cocked their head in unison, glanced at each other, and then Morrison continued, "Had anyone else come into the dining room at that point?"

"Nope."

"When did Mr. Cook arrive?"

Lizzie shrugged. Morrison clarified, "Were you there when he came in?"

Lizzie nodded, smirked and shivered slightly as if thinking about it was distasteful. Morrison asked, "Did he get a tray or did someone bring it to him?"

Lizzie glared at her inquisitor. "You been talkin' to Stein?"

Morrison put down his notepad. "Why?"

Lizzie drummed her long, bony fingers on the arm of the chair. "Cuz he asked the same stupid question."

Morrison followed up. "Why would Mr. Stein ask you that?"

"Cuz he's a knuckle-head."

Morrison could not help chuckling at the cantankerous old woman. "I don't know why Mr. Stein asked you, but can you answer my question?"

"Katie Mae took him a tray. She's his squeeze."

Morrison chuckled again as he wrote in his notepad. "Did Katie Mae join him?"

Lizzie looked to one side. "Hmmph. She sat with the chatterboxes. They act like their little goings-on is a secret."

Lizzie looked at Morrison with a sneer. "They ain't, weren't, foolin' nobody."

"Oh?"

Lizzie smoothed her dress. "Everbody knew about Katie Mae and that thug."

Morrison looked into her eyes. "Katie Mae have any reason to want Mr. Cook dead?"

Lizzie slapped her knees and howled. "Ha! She's the only one that DIDN'T want him dead."

Blakeley cocked his head. "Did you want him dead?"

The woman's face drew grim and her eyes piercing, Blakeley leaned forward to hear her answer. "Damn right I wanted to kill him. Many's the time."

"How'd you do it?"

Her face contorted with confusion. "Do what?"

"Kill him."

She howled again. "Aha! Wish I'd a dunnit. Nobody deserved it more than that swine."

Blakeley's eyes were as big as oysters, Morrison stepped in. "You know who did it?"

Lizzie raised an eyebrow and studied him as if deciding whether to trust him. "Everbody knows who did it. We all saw it. I warned him, you know."

Anticipation was swelling in Blakeley's chest, his eyes were ready to pop. Morrison frowned. "Who did it, Mrs. Dawson?"

"The ghosts, you fool!"

Blakeley grabbed his hat and slammed it to the floor, stood and turned his back on the wild woman. "Oh, for goodness sakes!"

Coincidently, the walls moaned followed by creaking or shuffling noises. Blakeley turned and stared at the walls. Morrison stared at Lizzie wondering if she was playing him or truly believed what she had just said. The spooky lady stared back with crazed eyes. Blakeley regained his composure. "Why would ghosts kill Mr. Cook?"

"Psst!" she huffed, "'Cuz he didn't have no respect for the dead. He mocked them once too many times."

Morrison was convinced. The woman who reportedly had once been a resident of the facility when it was an institution for the insane, was, without a doubt, either crazy, or the most ruthless murderess he had ever encountered.

Blakeley was visibly shaking with anger as he took his seat. Morrison followed up. "Anything else, Mrs. Dawson?"

"Can I go now?"

Blakeley was squirming in his chair. Morrison stood and declared,"That's all for now, thank you."

Chapter Thirty-Five
The Five Sleuthkateers

Next door to the north reception area was St. Jude's main library. The seldom used library could be accessed directly from the corridor or through the parlor next to it. And it also connected to the north reception room through a forgotten, ornate but inconspicuous wooden door. On this auspicious day, five over-curious resident sleuths were huddled behind the door straining to overhear the interviews.

"Shh!" Albert Stein insisted as he frowned at Walter Montgomery and Ralph Jacobs jockeying for position. Monty was trying to place a plastic water cup against the door to listen through, but his massive body was inappropriate for access next to Ralph and Albert also pressing their plastic cups against the narrow door.

Frank turned to see what White Feather was doing. The old Indian shook his head contemptuously as he tried to ignore the silly white men and their inept listening devices. He came as close to smiling as a crusty old wizard can as he held up his plastic cup full of water, dropped in his crystal, and then dropped in a piece of an Alka-Seltzer tablet to make the water fizz.

Frank whispered, "What's that for?"

White Feather whispered, "In the old days, we used the 'white water,' where the water rushes over the rocks. The frothing water flowing over the crystal produces images that a wizard can read, like the White Man's television or Iphone."

Frank got it. "But, without a stream ..."

White Feather smiled. "In the modern world, one may be forced to become ingenious."

Frank picked up a chair and quietly set it next to the wizard. "What do you see?" he whispered.

"Elizabeth Dawson." White Feather pointed at the door their friends were pressed up against, then he chuckled.

Frank leaned over and squinted. "What?"

"She spit on the floor."

Frank grabbed his mouth to stifle his laugh. Ralph and Albert glanced back. White Feather put a finger over his lips. "Sge."

His four accomplices turned to ogle him. "What?" Ralph whispered.

White Feather ignored his curious friends until they shuffled over to peer over his shoulder at the crystallized quartz sitting in fizzing water. "What's that?" Ralph whispered. White Feather raised a finger to his mouth to hush the irritating colleague and then whispered, "Morrison has started his questions."

Monty's eyes lit up and he took advantage of the opportunity to reestablish his position at the door. While his friends waited for White Feather's report, he tried his plastic cup again, first with the base to the door, then with the base to his ear. Frustrated, he carefully turned the door knob and pushed the heavy door open. The creaking door sent flashes of fright through the stealthy sleuths. They displayed outrage for their gutsy or, more accurately, klutzy friend.

They froze, held their breaths, and waited. White Feather studied his crystal for any reaction or any sign of detection by the deputy and agent. He whispered that they looked at each other curiously, but then Morrison continued his questioning.

To Frank, the creaking door, their scuffles, their whispers, were loud enough to be heard on the second floor. He was certain that it was only a matter of time before the lawmen raided the library and arrested them. But, for the five self-appointed, resident detectives, this was an event not to be missed and worth the risk.

With the door ajar, the voices from the reception area drifted into the library. Frank and Ralph rushed back to the door and jostled for position. Albert rushed over to slap the noisy, bungling fools on the backs of their heads only stirring them to rebel more stubbornly. The distinguished double for Woody Allen gave up and wriggled his skinny body against the larger men, knifing closer.

Nearby, the wizard focused on his modern contrivance for an ancient custom as quiet finally settled into the library stakeout.

Chapter Thirty-Six

4:00 P.M. Follow-Up with TJ

MORRISON WATCHED THE ELDERLY woman leave the room slowly, painfully, as if wading through thick air with feeble legs. Blakeley was pacing the floor like a flustered dog. Morrison shook his head as he watched the nicotine craving agent rub his lips with his hand. Morrison followed Lizzie to the door where he found a short, teenaged girl leaning against the wall just outside the door. "Are you TJ?"

"Yessir." The shy, nervous girl replied.

Morrison smiled and touched her shoulder. "Are you OK?"

A tear ran down her cheek. "Yessir."

Morrison patted her shoulder. "Come on in, we just have a few more questions."

TJ clasped her hands in front of her and dragged herself through the door with stooped shoulders and bowed head. Morrison nodded toward the nervous agent. "This is Agent Blakeley with CBI. He will be sitting in, if that's alright?"

Blakeley was irritated by Morrison's comment. TJ shrugged and waited for Morrison to indicate where to sit. He waved his hand toward the couch and she sat on the edge of the seat.

"I guess you overheard our interview with Mrs. Dawson?"

TJ looked up with sad, tentative, round blue eyes. "Yessir, some of it."

Morrison kidded her. "So, do you agree with her, that ghosts killed Mr. Cook?"

TJ snickered. "No sir."

Morrison smiled and chuckled. TJ giggled and relaxed slightly. Morrison tried to be gentle. "I know you have answered our questions already, but there are just some points I'd like to go over, OK?"

TJ took a deep breath. "OK."

Morrison and Blakeley dragged their chairs back over to the couch. Blakeley asserted himself. "When did you first see Mr. Cook that day?"

TJ looked down at the floor and started bouncing her legs with her feet. "I had taken the morning off for school. I came in around ten-thirty. I was supposed to escort the new resident to the dining room, but he had just gotten unpacked and wanted to take a shower and get cleaned up first. So, I left him and went to help one of the other residents to the dining room. When we got there, Mr. Cook was already there. I wheeled Mrs. Smith to a table and got her a tray."

Morrison took over. "Did Mr. Cook see you?"

TJ squirmed in her chair. "I tried to avoid him, but he hollered at me and motioned for me to come over."

"Did you?"

"No. I just ignored him. Acted like I didn't see him. Fortunately, Katie Mae came in and distracted him."

Morrison finished up a note and then continued, "Did you notice whether Mr. Cook had his tray and tea when you came in?"

TJ gave Morrison a blank look and then rolled up her eyes in thought. "Hmmm. No, I think Katie Mae took him his tray. I didn't notice ... no wait, yeah, he had tea. He held up his glass when he hollered at me."

Morrison nodded as he wrote. The poor girl's voice was trembling and it was clear she was very tense. He decided to try to give her a chance to relax. He leaned back with a slight smile. "Tell me about school. What are you taking?"

Blakeley turned and glared at Morrison. TJ shifted and took a deep breath. "Well, I'm only taking biochemistry this semester."

Blakeley's eyes bulged and he sat up in his chair. Morrison resisted the urge to make a note and then asked, "What's your major?"

TJ's eyes seemed to sparkle and her face lit up when she responded. "Pre-pharmacy. I want to be a pharmacist."

Morrison smiled and nodded. "Where are you going?"

TJ blushed. "CSU in Pueblo."

Blakeley jumped in. "CSU has a pharmacy program?"

"Pre-pharmacy. I will have to go somewhere else after I graduate from CSU."

Blakeley cocked his head to one side. "Requires a lot of chemistry, I guess."

TJ wriggled back on the cushion, placed her hands on the edge of the couch and started swinging her feet out and back again. "Yes, but I love chemistry. I love to find out what things are made of and mix up new stuff."

Blakeley jumped in. "Like strychnine?"

Morrison could see where Blakeley's questions were going. He leaned forward to regain control of the interview. "What do you know about strychnine, TJ?"

TJ's face grew pale and her eyes displayed her concern. "Is that what killed Mr. Cook?"

Morrison sat back and recrossed his legs and tried to put TJ at ease. "We think so, but I don't know that much about it. Have you run across it in your studies?"

TJ was not at ease. "No sir. I've heard of it, but all I know is that it is a deadly poison."

Morrison smiled at the nervous girl and changed the subject. "How long have you worked at St. Jude?"

Blakeley shifted contemptuously in his chair and wrote bold notes in his notepad. TJ pulled her legs up under the couch, straightened up, and clasped her hands together in her lap. "This is my third year here. I started my last semester in high school."

"You must like it."

TJ smiled again. "Oh, yes, I love it."

Blakeley shifted in his chair again, but Morrison pressed on. "Sounds like they try to work with you on your schooling."

"Oh, yes. There are a couple of us going to school and they are very flexible with our schedules."

"Morrison raised one eyebrow. "How responsive are they when you have a complaint? Did you ever have to go to them with a problem with one of the residents?"

TJ looked at him slyly. "You mean Mr. Cook?"

Morrison smiled. "Did you complain to them about Mr. Cook?"

TJ's eyes rolled up and she smirked. "At least a dozen times. I know their hands were tied to some extent. They talked to him and Deputy Crab came out and tried to straighten him out. It would work for a while, but then he'd just go back to his antics."

"It must have put you in a difficult spot."

TJ shrugged. "It put everyone in a difficult spot. Everyone hated him."

Blakeley blurted out, "Did you hate him?"

TJ tilted her head to one side. "I hated how he treated me and the others, but I felt sorry for him. I think he was lonely and frustrated. I think he felt trapped. St. Jude was his only option and I think he hated it."

"Do you know of anyone who hated him enough to want to kill him?"

TJ's eyes widened and she tossed her head as if overwhelmed by the question. "I guess there were a lot of people who hated him. But, I don't know of anyone who would actually kill him."

Blakeley continued, "If someone wanted to kill him, where would they get strychnine?"

TJ's eyes widened again and then focused. "Wow. That's a good question."

Her eyelids blinked rapidly as she was pondering the question. "Ms. Nujent keeps some prescription medicine in her pharmacy, but I can't imagine she would keep strychnine."

She looked at Morrison directly. "Isn't that used for killing rats?"

Morrison shrugged. "I think so."

"Maybe they keep some in maintenance or in the grounds shed."

Morrison raised his eyebrows. "Did you notice any-one from maintenance in the dining room or kitchen that day?"

TJ's eyes rolled up again. "Oh. Well, no, I don't think so. I was at school most of the morning. Besides, we don't have a maintenance staff, as such. Mrs. Barkley calls someone when we need them."

Morrison made a note. "That's a good suggestion, though. We'll look into it."

Morrison looked over his notes for a minute, and then turned to Blakeley. "You have anything else for TJ?"

Blakeley turned away from Morrison without answering.

Morrison smiled and stood up. He reached out a hand to TJ. "Thanks, TJ, you have been very helpful."

TJ jumped up and meekly took his hand. "Oh! OK, no problem."

As she disappeared out the door, Blakeley turned back to Morrison and smiled slyly. "Pharmacy, eh?"

Chapter Thirty-Seven

4:28 P.M. Sleuthkateers

WALTER MONTGOMERY AND RALPH Jacobs were crouching behind the ornate door that connected the library to the reception area straining to listen to TJ's interview. Albert and Frank rested comfortably in chairs placed on either side of the door and as long as Monty and Ralph kept their mouth shut and were still, they could hear the interview clearly. White Feather sat on the lush couch in the center of the room and observed the interview through his crystal submerged in a clear plastic cup filled with water stimulated by a dissolving piece of Alka-Seltzer.

He set down the cup and closed his eyes. As the girl and Morrison passed by the ornate door, Monty and Ralph scurried back to stay out of sight. Albert and Frank glanced at each other and chuckled at their clumsy friends. Monty was pleased and flashed a thumbs up. Albert smiled and nodded. Frank thought the interview had gone well and he felt hopeful that TJ did not appear to be a serious suspect.

Ralph poured water over their jubilation. "Pharmacy thing's a problem."

His friends' smiles faded as Monty spoke for them. "Oh, dear!"

They turned to White Feather for his take on it. The old wizard nodded his head. "The CBI agent made the connection. Morrison made a note."

The Sleuthkateers glanced at each other with silent stares. Albert pulled out his list and mouthed, "Katie Mae is next."

The spies scurried into position. Suddenly, White Feather raised his head to stare at the door. His eyes grew large and caught the attention of the others. They turned their attention to the door just as it slammed shut. The closing of the door was like a gunshot and sent Albert and Frank scrambling out of their chairs.

Like deer caught in headlights beside the road, they stood frozen staring at the door waiting—waiting for the raid they were sure was about to happen.

Chapter Thirty-Eight
4:30 P.M. Katie Mae

THE SLENDER, ATTRACTIVE, SIXTY-ISH woman sauntered into the room dabbing her eyes with a crumpled tissue. In the chaos of the event, Katie Mae and the Wilsons had escaped questioning in the original investigation. Morrison introduced himself and the CBI agent and invited her to sit.

She dropped down on the couch, crossed her legs, placed her elbow on her knee and placed her chin on her palm. Morrison detoured to the reception desk and grabbed a square box of Kleenex. As he started back, he thought he heard a noise and paused. There was an ornate door almost hidden between book shelves next to the desk. He speculated that it led into the library next door. He listened for a moment and thought he could hear faint whispering. Through the crack in the door, he could see the crossed legs of someone sitting in a chair with his back to the door. He smiled as he stepped over and pulled the door closed, then strolled over to set the tissue box next to Katie Mae. She gratefully snatched several tissues.

Morrison sat down and pulled out his notebook and pen. "Katie Mae ...?"

"Johnson." She answered hoarsely.

"I understand you knew Mr. Cook pretty well?"

Katie Mae blew her nose and straightened. "Oh, yes. I've known Benny for many years."

Morrison looked up. "You knew Mr. Cook before he moved to St. Jude?"

Katie Mae attempted a smile. "Yes. We worked together at the old hotel in Canon City. He was the doorman and I cleaned rooms."

Morrison made a note. "What was he like back then?"

"He was very distinguished and proper. Everyone liked him. The guests would ask for him personally because he treated them so well and they knew he would take good care of them and their luggage. He joked with them and they would go to him for suggestions about the local attractions. He knew all about the area and what to do and see."

Morrison studied her for a moment trying to be somewhat tactful. "Most of the residents here have painted a very different picture of him."

She huffed. "Shhhew. They just don't know him like I do. Benny would do anything for you. He's, he was, a very generous and warm man. But, when they closed the hotel, Benny took it pretty hard. He was never able to find anything else he liked, not like his position at the Hotel. Then he really took Ellie's death hard. I've tried to help him, but he's a proud man and he blames St. Jude for his ... for what happened to the hotel."

Blakeley was confused. "Why did he blame St. Jude?"

Katie Mae chuckled. "I know it don't make no sense, but you see this was a hospital originally. Then they tore down the hotel to make room to expand the hospital in Canon City. In Benny's crazy mind, if St. Jude hadn't been so old, they wouldn't have closed it and wouldn't have had to tear down the hotel to add on to the Canon City hospital."

She opened up her arms and shook her head. "Never mind that the owners of the hotel had been lookin' for a way to get out of the business for years. They'd have probably closed that old thang anyways."

Morrison took a moment to catch up his notes and then tried to get back on track. "So, did Mr. Cook act differently around you?"

She laughed. "Most of the time. When we's alone, he relaxed and joked around. We had some good talks and reminisced about the old days a lot."

"Tell me about Sunday."

Katie Mae glanced at Agent Blakeley and shifted on the couch. "Well, I slept over Saturday night. Benny didn't want nobody to know about us. He was funny about that. So, I slipped out early and went to my room. When I went to breakfast, he was there already and makin' a fuss, as usual. I joined Lizzie and the gals and I didn't pay no attention to him. That's what he wanted."

She looked down sadly at the floor. "After breakfast, I went up to my room and took a nap."

She glanced up and smirked at Morrison. "Didn't get much sleep that night, you know?"

She looked back down. "The next time I saw Benny was at lunch. When I got there, he was sittin' by himself kinda broodin' like. He looked so sad. He didn't notice me at first. I got him a tray and some more tea, and he perked up when I set it in front of him. I winked at him and his poor ole' face lit up and then I could tell he was embarrassed. So I went on over to fetch my food and ignored him as I strolled by and joined the gals."

Morrison made a note. "What happened next?"

"Well, not long after, little TJ escorted that new guy over to sit with Benny. I was sorta surprised 'cause TJ don't like Benny very much. He's always teasin' her."

Katie Mae giggled and lowered her head. "He grabbed her and asked her to get him some more tea. She wriggled loose, fussed at him and then stomped off to fetch his tea. Then Woody came in—that's what Benny called Mr. Stein."

Katie Mae paused to think. "I got busy talkin' to Trudy until Lizzie came in and Benny sang that stupid song and got her all riled up."

Blakeley interrupted, "What song?"

Katie Mae shook her head. "Oh, you know, that old song about that girl who murdered her folks a long time ago—Lizzie Bowden took a hatchet and gave her daddy forty whacks. When she was done with him, she gave her mammy forty-one."

Blakeley huffed and set down his notebook. Morrison nodded and made a note. Katie Mae continued, "Lizzie went ballistic and went after Benny, but Ruth and Marie managed to hold her back while Birdie came over to calm everbody down. Then poor old man Wilson pulled his tray onto his lap and drew attention away from Lizzie and Benny. While they was tryin' to calm Lizzie down, I heard Benny gaspin' and looked around and he was thrashin' about like someone was chokin' him. Lizzie jumped up and started shoutin' 'I tole you they'd get you,' or somethin' like that."

Tears filled her eyes and her voice trailed off. "And then he fell over on his tray ... dead."

Morrison paused to study the sobbing woman. After a moment, he stood and touched her shoulder. "We don't have any more questions, Mrs. Johnson. Thanks for your help."

Chapter Thirty-Nine

4:33 P.M. Scrambled Egg-heads

Swimming with fright, Monty and Ralph scrambled out of the library into the parlor and huddled at the parlor door to covertly scan the corridor. Albert stared into the eyes of White Feather while Frank studied Albert. White Feather glanced at his crystal, smiled and gave Albert reassurance. Albert strolled into the parlor and explained to Monty, Ralph, and Frank in a soft voice, "The deputy, Morrison, closed the door but apparently doesn't suspect anything. He went straight back to questioning Katie Mae."

Ralph complained, "With the door closed, we can't hear a dang thing."

Albert nodded resignedly. "True."

Monty felt something touch his shoulder, gasped, squeaked and spun around. White Feather slipped past him and approached Albert. "Found something."

Like puppies following their mother, the curious sleuths followed White Feather back into the library. They noticed a pile of books scattered on the floor near the center of the room and saw that White Feather had pulled them from the bottom shelf of the floor-to-ceiling bookshelf. White Feather squatted down in front of the vacated shelf, put a finger to his lips and whispered, "Listen."

Albert dropped to his knees and put his head close to the gap. The voices in the north reception room could be heard clearly. Albert looked at White Feather curiously, White Feather explained, "Crack in the wall."

Chapter Forty

5:00 P.M. The Wilsons

Mr. WILSON WAS SMILING with a gleam in his eyes, Mrs. Wilson was frowning with a glare in her eyes when they entered the northeast reception room. Sam Morrison tried to turn around Mrs. Wilson's attitude with his best smile. "Good afternoon, Mrs. and Mr. Wilson. I am Deputy Sam Morrison of the Wet Mountain County Sheriff's Office and this is Agent Miles Blakeley with the Colorado Bureau of Investigation."

Mr. Wilson beamed and shook his hand. Mrs. Wilson nodded glumly and whispered, "Let's go sit, Dear," and led her husband to the couch. As soon as they were settled, Mrs. Wilson held up her wrist, adjusted her watch, and studied the time. Morrison and Blakeley sat across from them. "We'll try not to keep you too long."

Mrs. Wilson smirked and laid her hands in her lap and sat straight, not leaning against the back of the couch like a proper lady from the past, like royalty trained from birth in proper posture. Mr. Wilson smiled pleasantly as he asked, "I'm sorry, do I know you?"

Mrs. Wilson turned her head and whispered, "No, Dear, these men are investigating the death of Benjamin Cook."

"Who?"

Wilson appeared confused and anxious as his eyes danced back and forth examining Morrison and Blakeley. Mrs. Wilson protested, "I really don't see why Benaford has to be here."

Morrison glanced at his impatient colleague, then leaned back and sympathized. "If you would prefer, I'm sure you could answer all of our questions."

Blakeley gasped. "What?"

Mrs. Wilson exhaled and seemed to relax slightly. "Thank you."

Morrison placed his hand on Blakeley's arm and whispered, "I'll explain."

She turned to her husband, "We are going to go back upstairs now, Benaford."

Benaford glanced around and smiled. "Yes, well good day, gentlemen."

"Good day, Mr. Wilson."

As the couple departed, Morrison turned to Blakeley and whispered, "Benaford has Alzheimer's."

In the library next door, the five Sleuthkateers laid on their backs fanned out like rays of the sun around the vacant bottom shelf of the bookshelf. The conversation in the next room could be heard through the crack in the wall only slightly muffled. Monty's eyes were wide with confusion written in them. "They are leaving?" he whispered desperately.

Ralph's frown called upon the many wrinkles in his face to express disgust. Albert put a finger to his lips and with the other hand motioned toward the parlor. The others obediently followed him into the large room and crowded behind him as they watched the Wilsons step into the elevator. "That's it?" Monty protested.

Albert calmly explained, "They don't need Mr. Wilson, Edith is escorting him back to the room."

Ralph snickered. Monty needed more clarification, asking, "She comin' back?"

All eyes turned to Albert to catch his nod.

When Edith Wilson returned, she was more relaxed, but her demeanor was formal and dignified. She sat pertly on the couch and inquired, "Agent Blakeley leave?"

Morrison dragged up his chair to face Mrs. Wilson more intimately and explained, "Smoke break."

Morrison opened his notepad. "So, can you tell me about what time you and your husband first saw Mr. Cook on Sunday?"

Mrs. Wilson took a deep breath and glanced up. "Well, I suppose that would have been around 9 A.M. at breakfast."

Agent Blakeley burst through the door and strode purposefully to his chair. Mrs. Wilson placed her fingers in front of her nose. He reeked of cigarette smoke. "Miss anything?" he asked as he sat down.

"We were just establishing when Mr. And Mrs. Wilson first saw Mr. Cook that day."

Mrs. Wilson repeated, "Nine o'clock or thereabouts."

Morrison was making notes and did not look up as he continued, "Did you speak with Mr. Cook?"

Mrs. Wilson huffed. "Pssst, no, thank goodness."

"How did you find him?"

"Benny was being Benny! He was haranguing everyone around him."

"But not you or Mr. Wilson?"

"No. Not this time. We sat in the corner with our backs to him."

Morrison paused to look the distinguished woman in the eye. "You didn't like Mr. Cook very much, did you?"

Mrs. Wilson chortled, "No one liked Mr. Cook."

"No one?"

Wilson shifted. "Well, perhaps Katie Mae. But even Naomi was embarrassed by his antics."

Blakeley cocked his head to one side. "Naomi? What's she got to do with it?"

Mrs. Wilson explained, "Naomi Johnson. She is his niece by marriage."

Morrison nodded. "Buster's cousin. She's the receptionist here."

Blakeley frowned and looked away as if disinterested. Morrison shifted in his chair. "So, when was the first time you actually encountered Mr. Cook that day?"

"It was just after noon when Benaford and I went down to lunch. Mr. Cook spotted us right away and hailed us over. I told Benaford to ignore Mr. Cook, but

Ben ... well, Benaford is trusting, so we wound up sitting at his table."

"He asked you to refill his tea?"

Wilson glanced up surprised by the question, but quickly recovered and stiffened. "Oh, yes! Lazy beggar."

Morrison waited; Wilson sensed he wanted more. "So, I went to get our trays first. Of course, Mr. Cook was not pleased. When I brought back three teas, I decided to make him reach for his." She shifted and crossed her legs. "Childish, I know, but it gave me some small measure of pleasure."

Morrison looked up from his notepad and smiled. "Where did you get his tea glass?"

She appeared to be confused. "Well ... from the tea cart."

Morrison sat back and crossed his legs. "Someone noticed that White Feather set a tea glass down and you took that glass to Cook."

Wilson frowned, covered her mouth with her fingers, and laughed uproariously. "Oh! How awful! I was so upset with Mr. Cook. Poor White Feather, he is such a nice man. He never said a word."

She dropped her forehead down on her thumb and forefinger and shook her head as she continued to chuckle. Morrison smiled and made a note.

Lying on the floor of the library next door, Frank observed the irritation on White Feather's face with the grins and snickers of his snarky friends. Ralph could not hold back. "Watch out, Chief, Edith has her eye on you." Ralph rolled up his eyes and fluttered his eyelashes, raised and waved his hands back and forth giving his imitation of a prissy girl. "He is SUCH a NICE man."

The Sleuthkateers enjoyed hushed laughter; even White Feather could not keep from snickering.

Next door, Morrison continued, "Were you there when Mr. Cook had his seizure?"

Wilson dropped her head. "No. Benaford dumped his tray in his lap and we went upstairs to clean him up. I heard about the ... incident afterward."

Blakeley cleared his throat. Morrison placed his notepad in his lap and stared at the impatient agent who then stated, "You had motive and opportunity to poison Mr. Cook."

Wilson glared at Blakeley with fire in her eyes. "You think I ...?"

Blakeley maintained eye contact until Mrs. Wilson looked down at her hands in her lap. "Yes, I guess I am a suspect. I detested that horrible man. I admit that I am glad to be rid of him."

Then something occurred to her and she looked Morrison in the eye. "But, you yourself pointed out that White Feather provided the glass of tea I gave to Mr. Cook."

Morrison blinked. She was right. Had White Feather slipped her a poisoned glass? Of course, he could not be sure which glass Edith would give to Cook.

Blakeley frowned and turned away. Morrison stood. "Thank you, Mrs. Wilson. I don't think we have any more questions for now."

The Sleuthkateers sat up and stared at White Feather. White Feather's stoic expression did not betray any concern. Albert glanced at his watch. "Time for dinner."

The big door at the entrance had not closed before Agent Blakeley lit a cigarette. As he blew out a voluminous cloud of gray smoke, he assessed the interviews. "That was a waste of time."

Morrison tried to hold his breath, then turned his head to try to siphon off air uncontaminated by Blakeley's addiction. The two men stood side by side but miles apart in their thoughts. Finally, Morrison offered, "You know, you don't have to drive over here for these interviews. I know it is a long drive and the interviews are so routine."

Blakeley turned to study his generous partner, then looked back at the distant Wet Mountains as he placed his cigarette to his lips. Morrison waited for an answer that would not come. At last, Blakeley finished his cigarette and tossed it down, stomped on it, and inhaled the crisp mountain air. "See you tomorrow."

Chapter Forty-One
6:30 P.M. Dinner

THE FIVE SLEUTHKATEERS WERE not interested in their meals as they ate somberly. No one sat in Benny's chair, but Frank thought he saw or maybe felt an almost imperceptible presence there. More like water evaporating off pavement. He noticed that the Indiankateer was also staring at the empty chair.

Careful not to mention his name, Frank asked, "So, White Feather, where do you think his soul is today?"

White Feather blinked as if waking from a distant dream but Ralph had a ready answer. "That sorry soul has burned to ashes by now."

Albert set the record straight. "I am aware of your take on it, Rudolf. I am curious, though, what White Feather can share with us."

White Feather closed his eyes. "Roberts, how many marks have you made on the round since the murder?"

Ralph stopped eating. "Round? What's that?"

Albert held up his hand. "Patience, Rudolf."

Frank visualized his calendar and remembered. "Two."

Ralph frowned. "Two what?"

Albert snapped impatiently. "Days."

White Feather nodded. "The elders, the wise ones, say that it takes the soul three days to a week to find the Nightland where the ancestors await."

Ralph huffed and resumed eating. Monty tapped his fingers together in the usual position of prayer while his eyes seemed to dance with delight. Apparently, Albert sensed that White Feather might not be in agreement with the elders. "Do you agree with the elders?"

White Feather smiled and raised an eyebrow. "You are quite perceptive for a white man."

Albert smirked. "I'm Jewish."

Everyone chuckled at his clever retort. White Feather pushed back the dangling feather from his face. "The ancestors believed that a man has four souls. They called them askinas. The conscious soul resides in the frontal lobe and is carried by saliva and exits the body with a man's last breath. The askina of the physiological life resides in the liver. It does not have an individuality like the conscious askina. It is that soul that tends to wellness and health and remains with the body for seven days before departing. The third askina resides in the heart and lingers for a moon cycle. Finally, the askina that resides in the bones and is carried in the marrow lingers for a sun cycle."

Ralph was curious as he swallowed and reached for his tea. "Which one produces ghosts?"

The others chuckled, but White Feather answered sincerely, "The first. The askina of consciousness may be confused at first and linger near the body before searching for the ancestors."

White Feather paused to let the information sink in. Albert was not satisfied. "But you have a different explanation?"

White Feather shifted into a philosophical approach. "Consciousness is a different state. It is not physical; it is not detectable. But it occupies an entity that is physical and detectable. That suggests that it may have been there before the entity and that it may remain in existence after the entity is gone."

Ralph snapped. "That's nuts."

Frank read "interesting" on Albert's lips; White Feather appeared to be quite satisfied with himself; Ralph appeared more interested in his dessert; Monty appeared confused. Frank was intrigued. "Where was it before it occupied the entity?"

White Feather smiled. "Now, there is the question."

Frank continued, "Is it floating around us, invisible to us?"

White Feather smiled knowingly at Frank. "Like time swirls around you in threaded contiguous circles?"

Frank remembered the apparition in Benny's old chair. "Perhaps it is ghost-like and sometimes visible under the right circumstances?"

White Feather shrugged. "Ghosts may be the residue from the connection of the consciousness to the entity."

Frank's mind reeled. "Whoa!"

Albert advanced the thought. "Like dust stirred into the air when an old tarp is removed from something it has been covering for a long time?"

White Feather stared at the Jewish Man for a moment as if digesting his alliteration. Monty was distracted by something more tangible. "The Wilsons have arrived."

Chapter Forty-Two
7:00 P.M. The Call

Had she not picked up on the second ring, Sam Morrison probably would have chickened out. "Hello."

"Hi, Sam," He managed.

There was no response. Morrison's heart dropped into his stomach. "How was your day?"

"Fine."

He could read into her terse response that she was angry or disgusted with him. *She knows about Darla!* he told himself. He took a deep breath. "I called to reschedule dinner ... if you still want to."

"Sure you don't have a conflict?"

She's definitely found out about Darla's visit! He tried to sound innocent, "A conflict? Oh, you mean the case?"

He heard her sarcastic laugh. "Hmmph."

He waited; she finally obliged. "I don't mean the case. I understand you had something else planned for the night you were supposed to come over."

"Yeah, well, I mean, no, nothing PLANNED." He gulped. He was not making it better.

Samantha confirmed that he was digging the hole deeper. "I thought you said you were exhausted."

"I was. Let me explain. Darla just dropped by. I didn't know she was coming over. I told her to leave. Nothing happened."

"Hmmph. Sure took a long time for nothing to happen."

Morrison took a deep breath. *Where should I begin?*

He heard Samantha take a breath too. "Look. We're no longer married. What you do with your life is your business."

"Well, that may be true, Sam, but you've got the wrong idea about Darla and me. There is no Darla and me. It's all a mistake."

"A mistake?"

"You see …" he started to try to tell her the entire story, but then realized how complicated it was. "Well, it's a long story."

"So, it's not the first time?"

Morrison gulped. "That's not what I meant. You see, Darla was involved in the Ludwig murder case. She was Jon Ludwig's mistress."

Samantha gasped. "Mistress? Oh, really, Sam."

"It's true, you can ask Buster. See, we found nude pictures of her on Ludwig's camera. When I confronted her, she admitted that she loved him."

"Mmm-hmm. So, with Ludwig out of the way, you decided to check her out."

"No! Nothing like that. The sheriff and I felt sorry for her and decided to give her the pictures and delete the files."

Samantha was quiet, he rushed on, "Well, she was grateful, you know? But, I guess she took it wrong. A little too grateful if you get my drift."

"Look, Sam, I don't blame you. She's an attractive girl."

"No! It's not like that, Sam. I told her in no uncertain terms that I am not interested in her. I think she understands now. Honest."

He could hear Samantha huff and then pause. He waited for what felt like a very long time before he suggested, "How about Friday night?"

Samantha begrudgingly accepted. "It's against my better judgment, Sam, but the kids do want to see you and I do want you to be a part of their lives. Friday night. Seven sharp. No excuses."

"Great! Thanks, Samantha."

She hung up.

Chapter Forty-Three

9:00 P.M. Walter Montgomery Alone

"GOOD EVENING, WALTER," ALBERT Stein proclaimed as he stopped at the door to Walter's room. Walter was deep in thought so Albert's comment startled him. "Oh! Yes, uh, oh yes, heh heh, good evening."

Walter's nervous, stuttering chuckle continued as Albert continued on down the narrow hallway to his room. Walter had been lamenting about his poor performance in the pool game with Ralph. Nothing was more frustrating for him than losing to such a lousy player. He could not understand why he could not regain the form he had as a college student in his fraternity. Even though he was older, the pool cue was light and the game was not strenuous. But maybe the magic of hand-eye coordination waned with age like all other things physical.

He opened the door to his room. It was the first room off the corridor in the southwest corner on the second floor. It was a great location, with a grand view of the Sangre de Cristo mountain range and was isolated and quiet. He flipped on the light. His room was not nice and neat like Albert's. Magazines cluttered the floor beside his recliner and the bed was unmade.

St. Jude's meager budget only allowed for house-keeping once a week. The residents were expected to take care of their rooms in the meantime. His room was not perfect but he thought the old ladies' rooms were worse.

He walked over to open the shades, but it was too dark to see the mountains and too light in his room to see the stars. He closed them and stopped by the small apartment-style refrigerator to pull out a beer. He kicked off his boots beside the vanity and turned to pick up the wadded up paper lying on the seat of the recliner and tossed it on the floor. As he collapsed into the soft chair, it creaked and moaned under his two-hundred-fifty pounds.

His cat, Gizmo, scurried out from under the bed and batted the paper wad playfully for a moment as his master screwed the lid off his beer and patted his knee. Gizmo obediently bit into the paper wad and jumped up on his lap. Walter rubbed the cat affectionately as he took a big swig of his beer. Gizmo dumped the crumpled paper on Walter's lap. Walter picked up the paper toy and tossed it back on the floor. Gizmo leaped to the floor to retrieve it.

Walter was proud of his cat's unique trick. How many pet owners had a cat that fetched? Unfortunately, he could not show off his brilliant cat since pets were not allowed at St. Jude. Fortunately, hiding when he was out of the room was another of Gizmo's tricks.

The pet and owner continued to play fetch while the owner finished his beer and dropped the empty bottle into a square, plastic trash can beside his recliner with the rest of that week's collection. Walter pulled the handle on the recliner and fell back signaling to Gizmo that play time was over. The cat batted the paper one more time and then leaped into the big man's lap and curled up for the massage that he knew he could count on.

While Walter attended to the cat, his eyes landed on the framed, aerial picture of his old clinic hanging on the wall. It provoked both a warm feeling but also a pang of regret. He suspected it was in ruin and falling down by now.

As a boy, he had worked beside his father with the animals. It was a bustling business back then. His father was a large animal veterinarian. That was when the valley was filled with cattle and sheep ranches. The business was so prosperous that Walter grew up accustomed to a life of privilege.

Walter's eyes found his college diploma next to the picture of the clinic. It had been one of the best times of his life. His father had given him an almost unlimited allowance enabling him to join the top fraternity and afford to keep up with his affluent frat brothers. Pool had been one of his specialties back then and he had developed a reputation as a shark.

But, sometime during his ten years in college acquiring his doctorate, the Wet Mountain Valley changed. Developers found the beautiful valley and started buying up the ranches and dividing them up into 7, 14, and 35 acre plots. A ski resort was carved out of the Sangre de Cristo Mountain directly west of the little village of Rockcliffe.

The dwindling business took its toll on his proud father who had grown up as an English gentleman accustomed to the finer things. When his father died suddenly of a heart attack, he left his only son ill-equipped to save the business. Walter learned budgeting and frugal living too slowly. For a time, after the clinic failed, he managed to survive as a resident vet at the huge buffalo ranch in southern Wet Mountain Valley. But, then he met Eloise Perdita Randall.

In addition to raising buffalo, the Elk Springs Ranch raised operating capital selling hunting packages to wealthy hunters from around the world. Walter fit in well with the affluent and his boss encouraged him to help host the big parties and barbeques on the ranch. When he was first introduced to Eloise Perdita Randall, Walter was his most charming self that night. "My, what a name!" he had told her, "I'm just going to call you 'Perdy,' cause you're so perdy."

She had giggled bashfully and stole his heart immediately. By the end of the two-week hunting visit, he magically stole her heart as well. After a short, long distance courtship, Walter found himself the groom in a grandiose wedding at the New England vacation home of the Randalls.

Perdy's father sat him down at the wedding and explained to him, man-to-man, that he expected his son-in-law to provide for his daughter. He made it clear that he would not be propping them up with his money.

Walter's salary proved to be too paltry to keep pace with Perdy's lifestyle. Ten tortuous, fiery years later, Perdy divorced him and left him destitute.

Walter pointed the remote control at his TV. His past was too painful to dwell on. Just as his future held no promise, finding a program worth watching was futile.

Gizmo purred contentedly in his lap as a single tear raced down his cheek.

Wednesday

Chapter Forty-Four

2:07 A.M. Four Score and Seven Years

Hours LATER, UPSTAIRS IN the parlor, another lonely old man pointed a remote control at a small, plain, black television set in the corner of the room.

The television was sitting unceremoniously on a cheap rolling cart with assorted VCR tapes cluttering the base of it. It was the only television in the home with a "tube" and that made it Frank's favorite. The glow from the television provided most of the light in the room but some light from the hallway cast long shadows across the room from behind him.

Franklin Roberts was sitting in a high-backed lounge chair in the room and could not be seen by anyone passing in the hallway. The TV flashed various shades of blue and white across Frank's face making him look very old and very creepy.

There was not much to watch at two A.M., but Frank could not sleep. It was not noise, worry, nor stress that was keeping him up, it was suffocating loneliness and futility that gripped him that night. Loneliness from being the only survivor of his family; no one to carry on the name or come to visit him; no hope of being remembered; no legacy to leave for posterity.

The truth was that he was not as isolated at St. Jude as he had been as a homeless vagrant. He knew some of the other homeless people that frequented the park near the bridge he had slept under in Canon City, but he had not bonded and established the type of friendships he had so quickly established at St. Jude.

In fact, the friendships and new life he was cultivating at St. Jude had the promise to be more rewarding than any over the last twenty years. But, perhaps this new taste of friendship and companionship had reminded him and had opened up the wounds of heartbreak and pain that he had suppressed and that had scabbed over as a homeless vagabond. Perhaps, this new life was forcing him to face his tragic circumstance.

A long healthy life had led him to this, but he mostly did not think about that. He was not a complainer. And although Frank had tried very hard, been very sincere and had always tried to make the best decisions at each point in his life, his efforts had not been rewarded with a comfortable retirement. Time had run out on him and he knew that he would spend the rest of his life destitute and at the mercy of charity.

Life was good when he had celebrated his seventieth birthday. He and his wife were living in a beautiful home in a nice neighborhood in south Aurora, Colorado. The home was paid off and they had a small retirement savings invested in the stock market.

Their daughter, their only child, and her successful husband were excited about their son's, his grandson's, graduation from high school. Frank was healthy and his job was not physically demanding so he was planning to work through his seventies. Then, as if a morbid portents, cancer took his wife after only a short battle.

The medical bills depleted their savings and forced him to refinance his lovely home. Then his daughter showed up desperate and announced that her husband was divorcing her. He could not turn her away since she and his grandson were his only remaining family. She moved in and for a while helped with groceries and some of the mortgage payments.

Then everything came crashing down in March 2000 in a series of devastating events. First, his daughter and grandson were tee-boned by a drunk driver and killed. Only two weeks after the funeral, the end of March, the value of his savings dropped by eighty-seven percent and most of the companies in his portfolio went bankrupt.

For eight years, he managed to work and make the payments on his mortgage and whittle away at his medical debts. Then the Great Recession of 2008 hit and the company he was working for folded leaving him out of a job, upside down on his mortgage and no savings. It took the bank two years before the foreclosure finalized leaving him homeless and broke.

Frank had had no choice but to turn to the streets. At eighty-two, he was too old to find a job so he spent the next five years living in a cardboard box under a bridge next to a park relying on homeless shelters for food and an occasional temporary bed.

Then, from out of the blue, Judy, the shelter volunteer had gotten him into St. Jude. It was a decent, clean facility, with friendly, helpful staff and he had already found a few friends. But, he knew that his good health meant that this final chapter in his life could be a long one.

These were the dreadful, haunting thoughts that stubbornly aggravated his mind that lonely night. He was not supposed to be up or out of his room, but the night aid had sympathetically looked the other way and had not bothered him. This small bit of independence meant a lot to him.

Most of the other residents were on medication or suffering from one of the many debilitating diseases that afflict the aged. His good health and quiet manner made him feel different and isolated from the general population at St. Jude.

The residents were friendly enough, and he had established a tentative relationship with the men at his dinner table but he was not sure he would fit in with them for long. So, tonight he had slipped into the television room to wallow in self-pity.

Frank clicked the remote searching for something of interest on the television. He stopped at the Weather Channel and stared at the chubby weatherman until he realized that he really did not care about the weather. He pointed the remote at the enthusiastic weatherman and clicked. One infomercial after another flashed on the screen until finally Frank stopped on an old movie. It was a black-and-white movie set in the civil war era. Abraham Lincoln walked up to a podium on a small, outdoor stage. The camera panned in as he began, "Four score and seven years ago ..."

Frank pondered the phrase "four score and seven years."

He calculated, *That would be eighty-seven years. That is my age! I am as old as the U.S. was when Abe Lincoln gave that speech.*

Frank contemplated the four scores of his life. The first score was the happiest he decided. His parents and grandparents had been so good to him that all the little selfish tantrums and childish demands now embarrassed him. If he could live those days over, he would not be that spoiled, self-centered child the second time around. He would try to live up to the generosity and all of the attention he had gotten growing up. He dreamed about returning with all of his current knowledge. He smiled at the possibilities.

The second score was fraught with great success in his career, but bitter failure in marriage. The second score of his life came crashing down with his company bankrupt and his marriage ending in divorce. He thought about what he would do if he could return to that time knowing what he knows now. He would not change anything at his work, but maybe he would not marry the same woman ... that woman! The thought made him feel guilty. What about his daughter? His wonderful daughter! Would it mean that she would never have existed?

He had tried to correct all of the mistakes of the second score in the third score. He had married more wisely and had kept his head down and worked hard. He and his second wife had saved their money and were well on their way to building a nice retirement. But as the fourth score reached its mid-point, tragedy struck again.

Throughout his life, every triumph had been offset with tragedy as if life was ruled by a median or average where successes had to be balanced against failures. It was hard to know where this episode in his life fit in that scheme. But, it did not feel like it offset the misfortune he had experienced as a homeless person. Frank did not want to think about it anymore. It was too painful. He pointed the remote and resumed channel surfing.

Chapter Forty-Five
3:00 A.M. Stacie Finds Frank

THE HALL CLOCK SOFTLY chimed thrice as resident aide
Stacie O'Neil found her newest resident asleep in the TV
room. She felt sorry for the kindly man. They had told
her that he had no family left. So, when she heard from her
daytime counterpart that Frank had made friends at dinner
and that he and the Cherokee resident, White Feather,
were seen visiting near the lake, she was encouraged.

Stacie pushed Frank's unruly hair away from his eyes
and sat in the chair next to him. She smiled as she watched
his eyes dancing under his closed eyelids. She hoped he
was having sweet dreams, but soon decided that more
likely he was having a painful dream. She gently touched
his shoulder and whispered, "Mr. Roberts ... Frank ...
wake up, Frank ..."

The troubled sleeper jerked awake, blinked rapidly
as he grasped for consciousness.

"Is everything alright, Mr. Roberts?"

Frank was breathing rapidly and starting to perspire
as he glared into the soft eyes of the friendly aide. "Oh,
... time to go to my room."

Frank leaned forward but Stacie placed her hand on his chest. "There's no rush. Want to talk?"

Frank sat back and took a deep breath as he tilted his head back and rubbed his face with the palms of his hands. Slowly his eyes returned to Stacie's and he smiled gratefully. "Sure, kid, what shall we talk about?"

Stacie giggled and tossed her hair as she sat back and placed her interlaced fingers in her lap, "I heard you had a run-in with Mrs. Nujent."

Frank shifted in his chair and frowned.

Stacie persisted. "What happened?"

"Oh, it was nothing, really. She caught me trying to use the red doors!"

Stacie raised an eyebrow curiously. "Why were you using the red doors?"

Frank shrugged. "I needed pen and paper and was going to Admin' to get it. Forgot about the red-door rule."

Stacie smiled. "You could've asked one of the aides. I'm sure they would've gotten it for you."

Frank chortled. "Nurse Nujent wouldn't have!"

The kindly aide frowned. "Why do you say that?"

"She said that 'pens are dangerous.'"

Stacie burst out laughing! "Dangerous?"

"Yeah, that's what I said."

"Then what did she say?"

Frank's temples rippled as he remembered. "She told me to 'run along, it was time for breakfast.'"

Stacie hissed and shook her head. "You should file a complaint, Frank."

Frank squirmed. She could tell that he was uncomfortable with that suggestion. "You NEED to file a complaint, Frank. She goes around upsetting all of the residents and no one ever complains. If she keeps getting away with it, she'll just keep doing it!"

Frank rubbed his nose with his forefinger. "You could tell them for me."

Frank's timid, pleading eyes touched Stacie's heart. "I can't do that, Frank, although I'd like to."

Frank held out his hands and shrugged as if saying, "So, there you are."

Stacie shifted in her chair and changed the subject. "I heard you have a new friend."

Frank frowned. "I do?"

"White Feather? TJ told me she saw you two sitting out by the pond."

Frank's eyes rolled up, then he smiled and refocused on the nosy aide. "Oh, yeah, the Indian. We sit at the same table now."

Frank looked down and unconsciously scribbled an imaginary circle on the arm of the chair with his finger. He wanted to be tactful. "Well, I wouldn't say we are close friends. We did have an ... interesting ... conversation by the pond."

Stacie smiled and probed, "What did you talk about?"

Frank shifted in his chair, nodded and explained, "He kept insisting that I SEE time."

"You see time?"

"Yeah. Well, he saw the circle I drew hanging on my wall."

Stacie's brow wrinkled as she struggled to remember the wall hanging. She had been in his room since he had come to St. Jude, but was embarrassed to admit she had never noticed a circle hanging on the wall. "What is the circle for?"

"Oh, it's nothing really. I just like to visualize the year as a circle with the months counter-clockwise around the circle. The traditional calendar confuses me. So I turned it over and drew a circle on the back and hung it up on the wall for quick reference."

Frank could tell from Stacie's blank look that she failed to understand the relevance of the circular calendar. Frank tried to explain, "Anyway, White Feather thinks that my calendar—the way that I visualize the year— proves that I SEE time."

Stacie laughed sympathetically. "Congratulations."

Frank chuckled, and then yawned grandly.

"So, what do YOU think, Frank?"

"I think I'm tired. It's time for bed."

Chapter Forty-Six

3:30 A.M. Stacie Investigates

STACIE TUCKED FRANK INTO bed and glanced around the room searching for his "calendar" drawing. She found it hanging unassumingly next to the chest of drawers drawn on the back of a regular calendar. *White Feather would've had to sneak into Frank's room to see the drawing!* Stacie thought.

"So this is what you 'see' when you see time?"

"Well, no, not exactly," Frank replied, a little embarrassed by the question.

Stacie walked over to sit on the edge of Frank's bed. "So, what do you see exactly?"

Frank took a deep breath and curled his lips repugnantly. He stared up at the ceiling, but Stacie could see that his eyes were unfocused. Perhaps he was looking at time now.

"Well, I see this huge circle, lying flat, suspended in nothingness. It looks something like an enormous vinyl record and the grooves are like threads. There are images of events flashing all around the circle."

Frank pointed to his left. "I can see images of old Thanksgivings over there, and Christmas over there ..."

"Where are you in relation to the circle?"

"I am in the midst of the circle where today is."

"So, you are standing on the circle?"

"Hmm. I don't think my physical body is there, it is just my point of view, so-to-speak."

"Are there signs or labels telling you where January, February, March, etc., are located? Like on your drawing?"

"No, I just know where they are."

Stacie slid off the bed and walked over to the drawing on the wall. "You labeled the months on your drawing."

"It's just a drawing, just for reference."

Stacie turned to Frank, questioningly. Frank elaborated. "So, I can see the previous month or the next month. When I imagine the year, I don't see words or numbers, just image streams."

Stacie turned back to look at the drawing again. "Very interesting, Frank. So, how do you think White Feather knows what you see?"

"I sensed that he had met others that SEE the same thing. In fact, he made the comment that 'others like me see EXACTLY the same thing.' To him that proves that we are seeing something, not just visualizing."

Stacie pinched her lips unconsciously. White Feather had made a good point! Something about Frank's vision was familiar. Maybe she had read something about it in her studies. She would look into it later.

"I had better get to work. I need to finish making my rounds. Very interesting, Frank. Do you think you'll talk to White Feather again about that ... or anything?"

Frank yawned grandly. "Oh, I don't know. He's kinda weird. But I am sitting at his table now, so ...."

"Who else is at your table?"

"Well, it's me, White Feather, Albert Stein, Walter Montgomery, and Ralph. Birdie calls us the Five Sleuthkateers."

Stacie laughed her delightful, easy laugh. "Sleuthkateers?"

Frank laughed with her. "We're investigating the Cook murder."

Stacie was intrigued. "Have any suspects?"

Frank was thoughtful for a moment. "Well, everyone is a suspect. Everyone had motive, except for Katie Mae, and everyone had opportunity. But, frankly, I don't think anyone I've met here, outside of Nujent, has the gumption to poison someone."

Stacie laughed again. "Why would Nujent poison someone?"

Frank smirked. "That's a good question. But, if Benny got on her bad side somehow ...."

Stacie patted Frank's hand. "Keep me posted, Mr. Sleuthkateer. Good night, Frank."

Stacie closed Frank's door and stood in the corridor for a moment in thought. She searched the archives of her memory for the reason that Frank's time images sounded familiar. Stacie thought that probably she had been exposed to it in one of her psychology courses.

A path of light flowed from under the door from the hallway. Frank lay staring at the dark ceiling. Abraham

Lincoln's face appeared in his mind. "Four score and seven years ago ...."

Memories of his first score streamed into his consciousness, *If I could go back,* he thought, *where would I start?*

Frank tried to imagine waking up in his bunk bed on the farm as a small boy. He wondered how that would work since he would have no memory of the previous day. Would that matter? Would anyone notice? Would anyone ask him about the previous day?

Frank imagined his mother coming in to wake him and telling him it was his first day at school. He would be confused, of course. How long would it take him to realize what had happened to him?

That's it! thought Frank, *The perfect re-entry point! It would be my first time to meet all my classmates and teacher. We would be on an even keel.*

Frank imagined the tiny room that had been his first grade class. Chubby Mrs. Benson was sitting at her desk facing the classroom. Seeing little Frankie and his mother enter the room she stood and donned a bright loving smile as she advanced to greet them.

Even eighty-one years later, the kindly Mrs. Benson could still put Frank at ease ... he drifted off to sleep.

As Stacie waited for Google to load, she debated what her search criteria should be. She decided to start simply with "I see time." The first hit was a book at *Amazon.com, I Was Blind, Now I See: Time to Be Happy.* But the second hit was *Rare Humans Who See Time and Have Amazing*

Memories. Stacie clicked on the topic, which brought up an article from *Discover Magazine.* There was a prominent picture of a shadowy form standing in front of an irregular circle divided into twelve colorful sections labeled with the months. The article began:

"The 'normal' form of the condition called synesthesia is weird enough: For people with this condition, sensory information gets mixed in the brain causing them to see sounds, taste colors, or perceive numbers as having particular hues.

"But psychologist David Brang is studying a bunch of people with an even odder form of synesthesia: These people can literally 'see time.'

"Brang's subjects have time-space synesthesia; because they have extra neural connections between certain regions of the brain, the patients experience time as a spatial construct."

Stacie looked up. *Synathesia! Well, I'll be darned! That weird old Indian may be on to something!*

Chapter Forty-Seven

7:15 A.M. The Life Path

FRANK AWOKE BROKEN-HEARTED! He could not remember very much about his dream but the feelings of grief, sadness, and sorrow lingered. *Whatever happened to feeling better in the morning?* he thought.

He had no desire to get up. There was no reason to, so for a few minutes, he allowed himself to wallow in the sad feelings. But over time, his sorrow turned to frustration; his thoughts shifted from himself to his situation and then to St. Jude.

The murder began to tickle his mind, a real life "who-dunit." The image of Mrs. Wilson dumping powder into the tea glass flashed into his head. He strained to remember the drink cart. Was there a brown box? He could not remember.

Then the curious appearance of White Feather beside her, placing a tea glass down that she slid over next to the glasses she was preparing. Were they in cahoots? Had White Feather surreptitiously slipped her a "Micky" for Benny?

The overpowering pain in his bladder interrupted the clever thoughts of the amateur sleuth and drove him to the bathroom for relief.

The relieved amateur detective dressed quickly in warm clothes suitable for outdoors. He wanted to take a walk; explore the grounds; think before breakfast.

He chuckled to himself. The last time he had tried to take a walk—to search for a way to escape—he had been distracted by White Feather.

Frank Roberts opened the tall, oversized door of St. Jude and descended the steps down to the concrete patio. The brisk morning air stung his face and brought back memories of his homeless life living outdoors in Canon City for five years.

How quickly he had adjusted to the warmth and shelter of St. Jude. He stretched out his arms and breathed in the fresh mountain air as he let his eyes feast on the beautiful peaks of the Sangre de Cristo Mountains just being touched by the morning sunrise.

As he exhaled, his eyes dropped to find the lush grass of the backyard leading up to the dark waters of the pond. That was when he noticed the pale, almost naked body of his new friend, White Feather, standing in the stream that flowed into the pond.

White Feather stretched out his arms to greet the Sun that illuminated his bare skin and made him look frail and ghost-like. His legs had to be freezing in the icy stream. Frank could barely hear the voice of the old Native

American chanting some strange prayer in his native tongue. The words sounded musical and entrancing. "Sge! A-'no-Gwo'" t^qa-'t aQnGa' yp'wi' Gan'o*f' ..."

The huge door behind him creaked and he spun around to see a short, skinny man stepping out dressed in sweat pants, tennis shoes, a bulky jacket, and a toboggan. Frank smiled. "Good morning, Albert."

The wiry little man jogged down the steps and then began his stretching exercises, "Good morning, Franklin."

"Have you come to join White Feather?" He nodded in the direction of the old man splashing water on his face and chest in the stream.

Albert glanced at the old Native American and chuckled. "Going to Water? Oh, no, too cold for my blood. Just came out for my preprandial jog."

"Pre-pran-dull?"

Albert raised his hands above his head, clasped his hands and began twisting and bending. "My before breakfast ritual, like White Feather's water ceremony."

Frank looked back at White Feather, "What's he doing?"

"Going to Water has been a tradition among his people for centuries. I think he told me it was time for the Green Corn Ceremony."

Frank nodded thoughtfully as he watched the old Cherokee turn and start chanting in a new direction. Albert continued his stretching, "He once told me that he had abandoned the sacred ceremonies of his ancestors in his youth after turning to follow the dark path of witchcraft."

Frank looked back at his busy, little friend. "Witchcraft?"

Albert wiped his sweaty face with the towel draped over his shoulders. "He told me that his actions had not been driven by dark intentions. In fact, he said he had turned to witchcraft for what was, in his mind, the noblest of intentions—to avenge his father's murder and to save the lives of an elderly couple that had taken him in and taught him the secrets of medicine and conjure."

Albert started jogging in place. "However, he said that over the years he had adopted old rituals and adapted them according to his own philosophy cobbled together from the philosophies of his ancestors and the philosophies of the modern world suited to his own interpretations. I think his religion has evolved into one of pragmatism and convenience."

They watched White Feather wade out of the stream and grab a bath towel to dry off. He looked invigorated and refreshed as he rubbed the water off his skin drawn tight against his bones. He seemed to be focused on the windows of the ancient building. Frank and Albert turned to look. The rotund silhouette of St. Jude Methodist Retirement Home's lovable cook, Birdie, was standing with her fists poked onto her large hips. She was shaking her head incredulously and they read "That crazy Injun" on her lips.

They smiled as White Feather pulled on his well-worn jeans and slipped into his handmade leather moccasins. He turned to put on his plaid flannel shirt and acted as if he was oblivious to the eyes staring at his back.

"He is too old and set in his ways to worry about critics watching him," Albert commented. "He knows he is the brunt of jokes, a tease for our curiosities, and a scary old shaman to most people, but he ignores that and follows his own path. I admire him for that."

"So, he 'goes to water' often?"

Albert headed for the path that circled the pond. Frank followed. "Yeah, pretty often. I've watched him from my room."

Albert turned and pointed to the hall window to the left of the corner window on the second floor. He paused and shook his head. "That was the empty room next to Benjamin's room. I have no doubt that he watched White Feather sometimes. That must have been very irritating for him."

Albert resumed his brisk walk. "I'm anxious to hear White Feather's take on the investigation and the interviews when we gather for breakfast."

"Me, too."

Frank turned to return to the Home and was startled to find White Feather standing beside him. "Oh! You startled me, White Feather."

White Feather was studying the gnarled tree in front of the bench by the pond. He questioned Frank, "When you think about your life, Time Man, do you see a long crooked path?"

Frank was surprised. He had never told anyone about the path! "How did you know about ...."

White Feather closed his eyes. Frank looked at the gnarled trees. "So do others LIKE ME see the crooked path, too?"

White Feather ignored the question. "Tell me about your path. Where does the path turn?"

Frank frowned. *Oh, great! Here we go again!* "Uh, look, White Feather, I was on my way to ... well, I mean, I have something I need to do."

"The point where the path turns is a re-entry point."

Frank was startled. "Re-entry point?" Frank studied the clairvoyant.

The clairvoyant smiled. "Everyone dreams of going back."

Frank shivered. This was making him very uncomfortable, "Yeah? Well ... I have to ..."

"Study the path, Frank."

Frank took a deep breath. "Okay. What am I looking for?"

"Each deviation in your path marks a point where you had a life-changing decision to make."

Frank studied the "life path" in his mind. Looking back, the path was straight for about the first ten years, then veered slightly to the right and a couple of years later veered right again. Around age twenty-two, it veered to the left and was straight for another eight-to-ten years. Then it veered right again. And so it went right up to the present ... and beyond! "It changes about every ten years."

"How far out does it go?"

Frank looked quizzically at the old sage, and then concentrated on the path beyond the present. The path was at the point of a left turn and then would proceed straight until around age ninety-nine where it turned right and then abruptly ended! "One-hundred-six!"

The Cherokee responded, "That's how much time you have left."

Frank shook his head and started to turn away.

"Study the tree, Frank!"

"Oh, good grief, White Feather." Frank looked back.

"The tree is a portal," the old Indian insisted.

Frank looked at his bare wrist. "It's time for breakfast."

Frank, zipped his jacket up all the way, lifted his collar flap and gripped White Feather's arm. They kept their silence as they sauntered back for breakfast.

Chapter Forty-Eight
8:06 A.M. Breakfast

FRANK YAWNED BROADLY AND stretched. Ralph commented without looking up, "Up late chasing women?"

Frank laughed. "Chasing?"

Ralph choked on his eggs spraying particles across the table. Albert, Monty and Frank cracked up at his expense. White Feather seemed lost in thought. As the levity settled down, Frank explained, "Couldn't sleep; watched TV until late, or rather, early this morning."

Monty's eyes twinkled. "Oh. What did you find to watch? An old movie?"

Ralph had resumed eating. "Snow, I'll bet."

Monty's brow wrinkled. "Snow?"

Albert snickered. "You know, Walter, when the stations go off the air, the static looks like snow on the screen."

Monty thought for a moment, then chuckled.

TJ startled them by sliding a sheet of paper onto the table and then rushed off to the next table. Ralph dropped his fork and seized the paper, studied it for a moment and then tossed it back onto the table. Monty's curiosity was killing him. "What did it say? What is it?"

Albert picked up the paper and announced, "It is the Sheriff's schedule for today's interviews." He scanned the page and reassured Monty. "You're not listed, Walter."

He glanced at Frank. "You're down for four P.M."

Frank's stomach quaked as he studied the back of the paper and wondered, *Why me?*

Albert laid the paper down. "I'm down for four-thirty."

Ralph shoveled a forkful of fruit into his mouth. "Start at three?"

Albert nodded. "We should meet in the library around two-thirty I should think."

Frank looked at the schedule. "Birdie at three, Nujent at three-thirty."

Ralph remarked, "That'll be good."

Chapter Forty-Nine

9:15 A.M. Nujent Collects Benny's Drugs

Frank stood in front of the elevator, pointed his finger at the up button and then realized at the last second that it was for the red doors. Frank paused in thought. Top Floor! Frank glanced around. No one was in the vicinity.

Frank pursed his lips, shuffled to the right and pushed the up button for the residents' elevator instead. The doors opened immediately and he stepped in and pushed number three, the highest resident floor, his floor. He clasped his hands in front of him and waited for the doors to close. He heard a thump as the doors started to close but just before the rubber bumpers touched, a slender hand reached through. Frank fumbled with the control panel looking for the "open door" button, but was too late, the intruder pushed the bumper back triggering the doors to reopen.

Frank turned to apologize for his fumbling only to be face-to-face with Nurse Nujent holding an empty cardboard box. Obviously disgusted to be in the elevator with him, Nujent announced in her most condescending tone, "Mr. Roberts."

Unfazed, Frank retorted, "Mrs. Nujent. I'm sorry, but this is the elevator for residents. Staff must use the red elevator."

Nujent was not amused. She huffed as she shifted the box to her left hand to free her right hand to punch the button for the second floor. Frank turned to face the control panel as the doors began to close again. Nurse Nujent shook her head and stepped back sulking.

"Oh," Frank whispered, "sorry."

Frank looked at the pert nurse quizzically. The impatient nurse shifted to one foot and ignored him. "What's the box for?" he asked.

She continued ignoring him. The elevator dinged as it settled on the second floor. "Where you goin'?" Frank ventured.

Nujent rolled her eyes as the doors opened and she stepped out, turned right and hustled off. While waiting for the doors to close, Frank decided to follow an impulse. He stepped out, turned right and caught a glimpse of Nujent turning right again and disappearing down the hallway.

Frank glanced around and then eased up to the hallway to peek around. Nujent was standing in front of Benny's room inserting her pass key into the lock. Frank smiled and thought to himself, *interesting*.

Nujent opened the door and pushed in. Frank slipped down the hall hoping to see what she was up to. He reasoned that if she caught him, Albert Stein's room was across the hall from Benny's and he could claim he was going there for a visit. He pressed his back against the wall and cautiously peeked around to find Nujent stooped over looking into the cabinet centered on the back wall of the room.

A clicking sound startled him. Albert's door creaked open a few inches and he could see one of Albert's eyes peering out. Frank peeked in Benny's old room again to find Nujent unloading bottles and packages into the cardboard box.

Then she carried the loaded box into the shared bathroom. Frank tip-toed across the hall and Albert opened his door to let him in. "Collecting his drugs," Albert whispered as Frank slipped past.

Albert pushed the door back but left it cracked open enough for the two nosy old men to peek across the hall. Nujent appeared lugging the heavy box, and Albert pushed the door closed quickly. "Wow!" Frank mouthed.

Albert tentatively checked, looking out again, and watched Nujent stride down the hall and disappear around the corner into the corridor. He shook his head as he closed the door. "Benjamin was hoarding a lot drugs it seems."

The skinny little man motioned toward the recliner for Frank to sit and then strolled over to a small, apartment-sized refrigerator and opened the door. "Soda pop, Franklin?"

"What've you got?"

"Whatever you want as long as you want Dr. Pepper."

Frank chuckled. "How'd you know?"

Albert took out two cans of Dr. Pepper, pulled two straws from a glass stuffed full of them and handed his friend a can and a straw. As Albert pulled open the tab of his can, he wriggled up onto the bed. Frank popped open his can, poked in the straw and enjoyed the prunes-like smell and the tingling fizzle on his face. "What do you suppose all that stuff was?"

Albert sipped his Dr. Pepper, smacked and licked his lips. "It's very curious. Mostly odd looking bottles or canisters. Some had homemade looking labels with Chinese and English lettering."

Frank raised his eyebrows. "I'm impressed, Sherlock."

The two sat in silence enjoying their drinks for a moment. Frank finally interjected, "Sure would like to know what was in those bottles and canisters."

Albert was still lost in his thoughts. Frank continued, "You know how to break into the clinic?"

Albert stared at him for a moment and then smiled deviously.

Chapter Fifty

9:45 A.M. Drawing Straws

THE EXCLUSIVE ST. JUDE Fraternity of Sleuthkateers had decided to meet in Albert's room situated near the southwest corner of the second floor. Albert shared the bathroom with Monty and the rooms across the hall were vacant so they were certain that their meeting would be confidential.

Ralph was the last to arrive, but the most impatient. "So, what's up?"

Albert raised his hands. "Patience, please, I will explain everything. Please be seated." Ralph glanced around the small room with only one recliner for a chair. Albert added apologetically, "Wherever you can find a place."

Monty had already grabbed the recliner. Ralph followed Frank's example and climbed onto the bed and leaned against the wall. White Feather chose to sit "Indian-style" on the floor.

Albert wriggled up onto the corner of the foot of the bed and glanced at his watch. "About thirty minutes ago, Franklin and I witnessed Nurse Nujent collecting Benjamin's medications from his room."

Ralph interrupted, "I bet that was interesting."

Albert smiled. "In fact, it was VERY interesting. Of particular interest were a rather large number of canisters with odd labels adorned with Chinese symbols."

White Feather's eyes popped open and he stared at Albert with doubting eyes. Ralph and Monty frowned curiously. Albert continued, "Franklin and I would like to know what is in those mysterious bottles and canisters."

Ralph stated his opinion. "Damn right!"

Monty got to the point. "How do we find out?"

Albert shared his plan. "We will need to distract Nurse Nujent. One of us is going to be sick and need the attention of Nurse Nujent."

Monty gasped and glanced around the room at his friends searching for signs of illness, but all he found were knowing smiles and chuckles. Still he offered, "Oh, dear. Maybe I could help. I was a veterinarian, you know."

His sweet naivety drew chuckles from everyone but Ralph. "Whose the unlucky ducky?"

Albert patiently fielded the question. "We will draw straws. It is, of course, just a diversion to allow the rest of us to investigate the clinic to see what strange medications Benjamin was taking."

Albert slid off the bed and scooped up five soda straws from the counter on the back wall. He secretly tore off part of one of the straws and then hid the modification in his hands as he rubbed them back and forth. He clenched his fist and carried the bundle of straws to Ralph. The contrary old man eyed the bundle intensely and then snatched one, snagging the others out of Albert's grasp and spilling them on the floor.

Frank commented, "Smooth, Jacobs."

The modified straw was easy to spot in the random stack on the floor. Albert could not contain his disgust as he reached for straws, but his action was superseded by White Feather's quick fingers plucking the short straw. He held it up, smiled and then showed it to Ralph. "Unlucky ducky."

The others were stunned albeit thankful that there was someone in the group who would actually want to face Nujent with a fake illness.

Chapter Fifty-One

10:15 A.M. The Caper

WHITE FEATHER STUFFED TWO slices of leftover beef lover's pizza into the blender tossing in a tomato for good measure and poured in six ounces of Parmesan cheese. While his special recipe was mixing, he placed his special bandanna in the microwave, set the timer and pushed START.

Then he filled a spray bottle with warm water, poured in some salt, screwed on the top, shook it vigorously and then stuffed it in his vest pocket. When the disgusting mixture in the blender was just less than pureed and appropriately chunky, the devious wizard shut off the screaming machine, grabbed the handle of the pitcher, removed the lid and sniffed. He felt his tongue and stomach contract as he gagged and slammed the lid back on the pitcher. He smiled satisfied—it was perfect.

After applying a clothes pin to his nostrils, he filled an eight ounce plastic cup with the awful blend and snapped on a plastic cover. Removing the clothes pin, he sniffed to confirm that the putrid stench was contained and set it on the counter. The microwave dinged and he removed the bandanna and wrapped it around his head, flinching against the scalding heat.

In some ways he felt bad about what he was about to do to the resident nurse. In the few weeks that he had been at St. Jude, she had been nothing but nice to him while tormenting all the other residents. She had been too nice. She was nice to him in the way he had seen mean people be nice to their dogs or cats or horses. It was belittling and made him feel subhuman.

It was as if she had adopted for herself the conscience of the white man and considered it her responsibility to be mean to her fellow whites and overly nice to Native Americans. White Feather saw it as an upside down form of racism. She was the anti-Benjamin.

He was ready. He picked up his cup of vomit, patted the spray bottle of sweat in his vest, tested his forehead below the bandanna to see if he was getting feverish and headed for the downstairs examining room.

White Feather rapped on the door to his four colleagues hiding in the ground floor antechamber next to the clinic as he strode by and headed on down the corridor leading to the exam room door. The narrow antechamber hallway where his friends awaited, led to where the north side door granted access to the outside of the building. It was a seldom used and mostly forgotten entrance to the building. In the center of the hallway, a never-used door connected to the clinic.

Albert slipped out of the antechamber to join White Feather while Monty, Frank, and Ralph waited by the locked clinic back door. Albert and White Feather stopped short of the open exam door to prepare for their charade. A red-faced White Feather ripped off the heated head band, spritzed his face with faux sweat, peeled the top off the cup, and held his nose as he took a big swig of the sickening mixture.

Albert gagged and took White Feather's arm to pretend to help his sick friend into the exam room. He hollered, "Nurse Nujent! We need help here!"

The nurse leaped from her desk and rushed over to White Feather just in time to receive the blast of faux-vomit over the front of her uniform. The smell of the putrid mixture prompted their stomachs to start convulsing giving them all an intense urge to vomit for real. Nujent screamed and looked down at the mess on her front. Albert offered, "Oh, dear, I'll get something to clean things up."

As he rushed into the clinic, Nujent guided White Feather over to the exam table while feeling of his forehead and cheeks. The smell prompted White Feather to vomit for real. Nujent was furious.

Albert raced across the clinic to the door connecting to the narrow hallway and antechamber and unlocked the dead bolt. Monty, Ralph and Frank rushed in. Then Albert threw open the door to the small corner closet to retrieve the mop and bucket. On his way back to the exam room, he grabbed an armful of towels.

When Albert burst back into the exam room, he found Nujent stripped down to bra and panties looking at her watch while White Feather sat looking pitiful on the exam table with a thermometer sticking out of his mouth. Albert stealthily twisted the button on the clinic door to lock it and then shut it and set down the mop bucket to cover the noise. Nujent directed Albert to sop up the mess with the towels while she checked her watch again.

Albert, the mild-mannered gentleman, became a wild, bungling madman cleaning up the mess while making an even bigger one. His wild antics successfully drove the fussy nurse into a frenzy.

Meanwhile, in the clinic, Ralph was busy searching the cabinets along one wall and Monty was checking under tables and desks. Frank reminded his cohorts, "It is a cardboard box about one-and-one-half feet by two feet square. Ralph corrected him. "That's a rectangle."

Frank discovered the box carelessly stuffed in a small closet in the back corner of the clinic. "Found it!"

Monty was by his side immediately and started rifling through its contents. Ralph pushed in and snatched one of the canisters with a Chinese label. Frank was scanning the contents not sure what he was looking for but hoping something would pop out at him.

They heard the door to the exam room and then Nujent scream, "Who locked this door?" The three sleuths in the clinic froze for a moment, looked at each other, snickered and then shoved the box back into the closet, missing the canister in Ralph's hand.

Quickly, the three burglars slipped out of the clinic, quietly shut the door and then exited the antechamber and headed down the corridor. As they approached the dining hall, Ralph burst out laughing. The others frowned at him and then discovered he was reading the label on the purloined canister. He read it out-loud, "Take two tablespoons with water two hours before sex."

Ralph's face contorted into a grimace as he laughed harder barely managing to declare, "Chinese Viagra!"

Chapter Fifty-Two
12:10 P.M. Dining

Monty and Frank were picking at their food in silence. Ralph was scarfing down his vittles in his usual voracious, noisy manner when Albert and White Feather finally arrived for lunch. White Feather was distant as he set down his tray and adjusted the makeshift bandage wrapped around his forehead. Albert explained, "The bandanna he used to simulate a fever was too hot. It scalded his forehead. Fortunately, Nujent was so flustered she did not notice the blisters popping up."

The four caper-buddies chuckled at poor White Feather's expense and then Albert apologized. "We're sorry, Ugidahli Unega. I'm sure you are in great pain. We appreciate your sacrifice."

White Feather sat down and began eating, ignoring his friends. Albert explained, "Quite ingenious really. The headband was for raising his temperature. He even added sweat to look like he was running a fever. The putrid mix was to provide vomit." Monty giggled at the cleverness of his friend.

Ralph was unsympathetic. "Worked. Now you're really sick."

The old friends laughed loudly as the cook, Birdie, approached. "What happened to you, White Feather, you look terrible."

The injured Injun did not look up. "Bumped my head."

"You're gonna have to be more careful. Can I get you an aspirin or anything?"

White Feather shook his head no. Albert interjected, "Nurse Nujent has provided him with a fine assortment of medications."

The old friends laughed again at their poor friend. Birdie sighed, "You old farts are hopeless."

Albert changed the subject. "Ready for your interview, Mrs. Beaudreau?"

"I declare, Mr. Stein, will you ever call me Birdie like everbody else?"

Albert smiled kindly. "I apologize Mrs. Birdie."

Birdie snickered. "I guess I'm ready. You ready for yours?"

Albert nodded. "The innocent have no fear of the law."

Ralph coughed.

Birdie shook her head and walked to the next table. Ralph slipped the "Chinese Viagra" canister to Albert under the table. Albert held it in his lap and read the label. He chuckled and looked up to find his friends anxiously awaiting his reaction. He turned to White Feather. "It seems that our old, departed friend was taking something for sexual enhancement."

He passed the canister to White Feather under the table. The old wizard read the label and turned it around and around in his hand. Then he removed the cap and raised it to his nose to smell. His friends gasped. "Keep it down!" Monty warned as he checked all around for witnesses.

Undeterred, White Feather pinched some of the powder and touched it to his tongue. After screwing the lid back on, he set the canister down and bolted up straight in his chair. Immediately, his eyes widened, his face grimaced and he started spitting and coughing. He grabbed his neck with both hands and flailed around for a moment. Then he stopped and smiled deviously at his friends. His action drove his friends to uncontrollable hilarity.

White Feather smiled proudly after his little prank. Frank was astounded. *So, he has a sense of humor after all.*

Chapter Fifty-Three

2:55 P.M. Birdie's Interview

THE SLEUTHKATEERS MINUS WHITE Feather waited quietly, stretched out on the floor of the ground floor library, side by side, with the tops of their heads near the bookcase. They had removed the books from the bottom shelf where the acoustic anomaly, the crack in the wall, enabled them to hear the interviews in the adjacent room. Ralph had discovered that a short stack of books made a dandy pillow.

It was 2:35 P.M. and the fifth member of the sleuth club was waiting in the north reception room. Agent Blakeley's voice echoed in the corridor as he related some wearisome story to his partner, Deputy Morrison. The stealthy Sleuthkateers listened intently to the men of law enter the reception room next to the library.

"Good afternoon, White Feather. What happened to your head?" It was Morrison's voice.

White Feather was sitting on the plush couch and held out a canister as Deputy Morrison approached. Blakeley protested, "You again?"

Morrison accepted the canister, "What have you got there?"

White Feather remained quiet as Morrison and Blakeley read the label. The label on the canister was a simple, home-made gummed label most likely printed on a PC inkjet printer. Chinese characters lined the left column of the label. "Zhuàngyáng jì" was printed in bold letters across the top with "Dr. Zhang Wei" printed below. Across the bottom, in English, "Take two tablespoons with water two hours before sex." Blakeley's eyes widened and he gasped as Morrison chuckled and looked at White Feather. "What is this?"

White Feather stood. "From the victim's room."

White Feather held up his hand to stop Morrison from asking the obvious question. As he walked by the curious deputy, he suggested, "Ask Nurse Nujent about it. It didn't come from me."

Blakeley began, "Where did you get ..." Morrison stopped him. "I think I know."

The happy, enthusiastic voice of Birdie rang out from the reception room entry startling the covert group in the library and the lawmen alike, except for Ralph Jacobs who continued to snore. Deputy Morrison greeted the grand lady of the kitchen, "Good day, Birdie. How are you this afternoon?"

Birdie waddled across the room and dropped on to the couch gasping. "Whew, busy day."

She fanned herself with a stained kitchen towel and blew unruly curls from her eyes. Blakeley glared at the happy woman who returned his glare with a raised eyebrow. "You again?"

Morrison searched the walls for the switch for the overhead fans. Birdie frowned. "What chu looking for, Deputy?"

"The switch for the fans."

Birdie rolled off the couch and strolled purposefully across the room to where an obscure panel of switches was mounted on the wall beside the outside entrance to the room. She flipped the middle switch, wiped her face with her towel and returned to her seat. The fans buzzed and then slowly began turning.

Morrison sat down, opened his notebook and began. "We'll try not to take up too much of your time, Birdie. Just need some clarification on a few things."

Birdie raised her chin and fanned her sweaty neck. Morrison rifled through his notebook and found the page he was looking for. "Do you ever fix Chinese food for the residents?"

Birdie stopped fanning herself and studied Morrison. "Chinese? Do I look Chinese to you?" She laughed enthusiastically.

Blakeley continued his glaring stare. Morrison chuckled. "The coroner found signs that Benny had been eating something containing a variety of herbs and stuff sometimes found in Chinese concoctions."

Birdie looked concerned. Morrison tried to put her at ease. "There were no signs of strychnine nor the odd mixture in the plate or tea glasses. So, he must have ingested the poison before he came to lunch, or by some other means."

Morrison looked up from his notepad. "Do you know if Benny was taking any medications?"

Birdie resumed fanning her face with the cloth. "I wouldn't know about that, but our residents are elderly and most take somethin'. Nujent would know."

Morrison nodded and handed her a list of the odd items from the lab report on the contents in Benjamin Cook's stomach. "Got any idea what recipe might have these ingredients?"

Birdie wrinkled her nose and placed one hand over her heart as she held out the list at arm's length. Her mouth moved slightly as she read the list. She studied it for a moment then handed it back to Morrison, "Not in my recipe book. So, it wasn't the rat poison?"

Morrison folded the paper and stuffed it in his shirt pocket. "Apparently not."

"Well, that puts a new wrinkle in it."

Morrison raised his eyebrows and nodded.

Chapter Fifty-Four

3:30 P.M. Nurse Nujent's Interview

Waiting impatiently in the first floor library, the Sleuthkateers checked their watches and then took up positions for the next interview. They heard the hasty, determined steps of Nurse Nujent coming down the hallway from her office promptly at 3:30.

Morrison stood to greet the stern woman when she barged into the room. "Good afternoon, Nurse Nujent. I am Deputy Morrison of the Wet Mountain County Sheriff's Office and this is Miles Blakeley with CBI."

Without comment, Nujent marched across the room and dropped onto the couch. She handed Morrison a typed list then crossed her arms and waited.

Morrison studied the list. It was an inventory of items collected from Benjamin Cook's room. Morrison noted the nine bottles of "A Chinese Concoction," and then handed the list to Blakeley.

Morrison readied his pencil and began. "How well did you know Mr. Cook?"

"Not well. I met him when he came by for the initial routine examination."

Morrison smiled. "Did he pass?"

Nujent frowned. "Pass?"

Morrison clarified. "Your examination."

Nujent shrugged. "He was healthy enough for someone his age."

Morrison made a note as he asked, "Was he taking any medications?"

Nujent huffed as if he had asked a silly question. "Lisinopril for blood pressure, Probenecid for gout."

Morrison looked up. "Could you spell those for me?"

She did, then pointed at the inventory. "And some other odd medications and drugs he neglected to disclose."

Blakeley jumped in. "Was he taking anything with strychnine in it?"

"Not that I know of."

Morrison followed up. "Where would someone get strychnine?"

Nujent slanted her head and raised an eyebrow. "You don't think they got it from the rat poison you found?"

Morrison explained, "The lab said there wasn't enough active poison in the box to have that kind of an effect."

Nujent smirked. "I wouldn't think so."

"And, oddly enough, no strychnine was found on his plate or in his tea glass."

Morrison handed her the list of odd ingredients from the lab's report. "Recognize these ingredients? They were in Cook's stomach in addition to the food, tea, and strychnine."

Nujent studied the odd mix of herbs and chemicals. Slowly she raised her head as her eyes gazed at the floor. "Could I keep this?"

Morrison nodded. "Recognize something?"

Nujent blinked and glanced at him. "It looks familiar, but I can't place it; maybe some bizarre alternative medication. Residents are supposed to keep me apprised of their medications. I'm sure Mr. Cook never mentioned anything like this, but I will look into it."

Morrison scribbled a note. "Do you keep strychnine or any medications in the clinic that contain strychnine?"

Nujent leaned her head to one side. "Years ago, you'd find strychnine in all sorts of things. It was once thought to be a performance enhancing drug and given to athletes; it was once used as an aphrodisiac in Oriental cultures."

She threw out her hands in disgust. "You name it!"

Morrison studied her. She shifted uncomfortably. The bottle in his pocket with Chinese symbols came to mind. Nujent continued, "This is an old building. It has had many functions. When I came back, I rounded up all the old drugs that I could find and disposed of them."

Morrison made a note, and then realized something. "Came back?"

Nujent's eyes betrayed her. "Well, I mean, I have been to this facility before. It was a hospital, you know, before it was a retirement home."

Morrison's detective instincts kicked in. "It was also a mental facility."

Blakeley's interest was stirred. Nujent tried to force a smile. "Yes ... I know."

Morrison tried to guess her age. "Were you ever here then?"

Morrison noted her red face and the hint of perspiration on her brow. "I was very young, but I did work here as a nurse's aide as a teenager for a short time."

Morrison's head flooded with questions. "When was that?"

Nujent's eyes rolled up in thought. "Well, I think I was seventeen or eighteen, so 1945, I guess."

Morrison did the math. He studied the stern woman's face. She couldn't be eighty-seven! He would have guessed she was in her sixties or seventies maybe.

Blakeley leaned forward and rested his elbows on his knees. Morrison was flabbergasted by the revelation. "Was Lizzie Dawson there then?"

Nujent shifted in her chair and stared at the floor. "Possibly, I guess."

Morrison scribbled in his notebook. "You were a nurse's aid?"

Nujent took a deep breath. "Yes."

Morrison looked up. "Were they using strychnine then?"

Nujent shrugged. "I have no idea."

Morrison studied her. He sensed she was hiding something, or perhaps her time in the institute was traumatic for her. He had heard there was abuse of patients during that time, so maybe it was natural for her to want to avoid revealing she had any involvement. Morrison sat back and crossed his legs. "What made you want to come back to this building?"

Nujent glanced at him with wet eyes and then looked away. "I needed a job ... there was an opening."

"Have you always lived in this area?"

She took a deep breath. "I moved away to go to college in New York."

"Is that where you got your nursing degree?"

"Yes."

Nujent snapped her head around toward the south wall, held up her hand and listened intently. Blakeley quizzed, "What is it? Hear something?"

Next door, Albert placed his hand over Ralph's nose and mouth to squelch his snoring. Ralph opened his eyes wide and looked around. Albert whispered, "You're snoring."

Nujent and the lawmen listened intently for several seconds. Morrison tried to hide his amusement. "Probably rats."

Nujent glared at him and then remarked slyly, "Where's the strychnine when you need it?"

Morrison was shocked by her uncharacteristic humor. Even Blakeley snickered. Morrison raised an eyebrow as he noted to himself, uncharacteristic for the agent nicknamed "Smiles" behind his back.

"You mentioned that strychnine was once used in Oriental potions. On your list, you have nine canisters of a "Chinese Concoction." Know what was in those?"

Nujent shrugged. "Not yet."

Morrison nodded. "I'd like to have one to send to the lab."

Nujent nodded. "Of course."

Chapter Fifty-Five
4:00 P.M. Roberts Interview

With sad faces, his friends patted him on the back as if sending him off to the gallows. It was Frank's turn in the interview chamber.

Frank felt his hand trembling as he shook hands with Deputy Morrison and Agent Blakeley. Morrison smiled and invited him to sit on the cushy couch. Frank leaned back and crossed his legs hoping the power gesture would calm his nerves.

Morrison began the interview. "So, Mr. Roberts, you are the new guy at St. Jude?"

Frank nodded. "Yes, sir."

"How do you like it so far?"

Frank shrugged. "It is a very nice place. The Cook thing was ..."

Morrison understood. "I'm sure it was a traumatic start."

Frank nodded. Blakeley yawned, Morrison flipped open his notebook. "We only have a few things to go over."

Frank strained to see if he could hear his bungling friends in the room next door. He could not.

Morrison asked, "You were sitting next to Mr. Cook that day?"

Frank nodded. Morrison continued, "Were you the first person to join Mr. Cook? Tell us about that."

Frank studied the floor as memories of that fateful event streamed into his mind. "TJ escorted me to the dining room and asked me where I wanted to sit. I didn't really know so I just popped off 'window seat.' The only table by the window that was not completely occupied was Benny's. He was all alone at the time. I didn't know him then so I suggested sitting with him. TJ tried to talk me out of it, but I resisted thinking she was just prejudiced, maybe."

Morrison interrupted, "Did he have his tray and tea at that point?"

Frank glanced up at him and then back down to the floor, "Yes. He was eating and had emptied his glass of tea."

Morrison nodded. "Go on."

"TJ was introducing me when Benny grabbed her and pulled her over to sort of hug her. She was furious with him, but he ignored that and gave her his glass to refill."

Frank looked up. "Which she did, but was careful when she returned to not get too close to him."

Morrison cocked his head to one side. "Did she protest when Mr. Cook grabbed her?"

"Oh, yes, she scolded him and told him to never do that again."

"How did Cook respond?"

"He just laughed."

As the interview proceeded, Frank noticed that neither Deputy Morrison nor Agent Blakeley were taking any notes. Perhaps he was not telling them anything new.

There was a knock on the door. It was Nurse Nujent. Frank recognized the two canisters she brought in as the same Chinese concoction Ralph had stolen from the clinic. She gave them to Morrison who handed one of the canisters over to Blakeley, "Thanks. I'll let you know what we find."

Nujent frowned. "Can I talk to you, privately?"

The two slipped out into the hallway. Frank could hear Nujent whispering, "I inventoried nine bottles."

Morrison responded, "Yes, I noticed that on the list."

"Now there are only eight."

Frank noticed Morrison glance at him and instinctively touch his pocket as he asked, "How do you account for that?"

"Stein and White Feather were in the clinic this morning. White Feather feigned a fever and made a mess to distract me. Stein was alone in the clinic where I had Cook's medications stored."

Morrison clarified, "You think they conspired to take the bottle?"

There was no answer from Nujent. Morrison followed up. "What would they want with it?"

"Beats me."

Morrison was quiet for a moment, then replied, "Let me look into it. I appreciate you're letting me know."

Morrison returned to the room and Frank tried to act nonchalant. Morrison sat down and reopened his notebook. "I've been told that you are a keen observer and that you may have seen something that others missed."

Frank was surprised. "Who said that?"

Blakeley snorted in contempt and sat back. Morrison shrugged. "Think about it. Do you remember anything that was subtle or possibly has gone unnoticed?"

Frank shook his head as he strained his brain for something to offer. Mrs. Wilson pouring a white powder into Benny's tea, then taking him a glass that White Feather had given her flashed into his head. But, they had already determined that the poison did not come from the tea or food. He felt under pressure to come up with something. "I thought it odd that Mr. Cook knew so much about the Institute for the Insane. And I wondered what he might have done that made Lizzie so concerned about the ghosts."

Morrison studied the old man for a moment and then made several notes in his notepad. "Interesting."

Morrison shifted in his chair. "You think Cook may have had a prior connection to Elizabeth?"

Frank felt vindicated. "Maybe. Just seems curious why he would know so much about the history of this place."

Morrison raised his eyebrows and tilted his heard to one side. "Anything else?"

Frank shook his head. "Can't think of anything else."

Chapter Fifty-Six

4:30 P.M. Stein Interview

As Albert Stein entered the reception room, Morrison admired the old retired journalist's quiet, dignified, and reserved countenance. "Good afternoon, Mr. Stein, have you met Miles Blakeley with CBI?"

Stein nodded toward Blakeley. "Not formally."

Blakeley turned away impatiently, sat and crossed his legs in a huff. Morrison motioned toward the couch. "Please have a seat. "

Stein saluted with two fingers and shuffled over to the couch. He exhibited no sign of concern or nervousness as he sat and crossed his legs. Morrison noticed him stare at the canister sitting on the table that Nujent had brought to him. Morrison picked up the medicine bottle. "I assume you have seen this?"

Blakeley turned to frown at Morrison. Stein nodded. Morrison asked, "What do you make of it?"

Stein responded, "It appears that Benjamin was anxious to impress Mrs. Johnson."

Morrison chuckled. "Have any idea what might be in it?"

"I am planning to Google it but have not yet."

Morrison nodded and placed the canister back on the table. "You've had some time to think about Mr. Cook's poisoning. Have any theories?"

Albert Stein sighed. "Although there would appear to be plenty of suspects with plenty of opportunity, I just don't know anyone here at St. Jude that I believe would have the resolve to pull it off."

"Not even Elizabeth Dawson?"

Stein chuckled. "Not even Elizabeth. I think that she truly believes ghosts took care of Benjamin for her."

Morrison smirked. "Is that the consensus of the Sleuthkateers?"

Albert Stein's eyes twinkled and he smiled slyly. "Not exactly."

Blakeley was confused. "Sleuthkateers?"

Morrison put up his hand. "I'll explain later."

He turned back to Stein. "What do your compadres think?"

The old gentleman recrossed his legs. "Actually, I'm not sure anyone has narrowed his suspicions to a single culprit, but Elizabeth and Nurse Nujent would probably be at the top of their list."

Morrison tilted his head. "Not Birdie or Mrs. Wilson?"

Stein rolled his head. "Perhaps Mrs. Wilson. She is strong enough, clever enough, and like all of us, she had opportunity and motive. But, in my opinion, Mrs. Wilson would be more likely to stand up to Benjamin mano a mano than to take the cowardly approach of poisoning him."

Ponderous silence claimed the moment. Morrison felt he understood where Albert Stein was coming from and they were on the same page. "Makes sense. By the way, we have determined that the poison was not administered in his drink or food."

Stein was not surprised. Morrison suspected he had heard this information from next door. But Stein asked, "You managed to test all five glasses he used?"

Morrison squinted. "Five?"

Stein explained, "When Katie Mae took him his tray, he already had a glass of tea. It was empty and she replaced it. That was empty when TJ arrived with Franklin and she got him another one. Mrs. Wilson brought him a fourth glass and Mrs. Beaudreau brought him the fifth glass."

"So you don't think the same glass was refilled each time?"

Stein considered the possibility, then answered, "Not likely. It would be easier to just grab another glass already filled."

Morrison looked at his partner, then back to Stein and smiled. "So, we can't rule out someone poisoning his glass after all."

Stein surprised the deputy further. "Did you test his microwave?"

"Cook had a microwave?"

Stein smiled slyly. "He didn't get to be that large by eating the portions served in the dining room. I often smelled delectable aromas coming from his room in between meals."

Morrison made a note and commented, "Might account for the odd items found in his stomach."

Stein nodded his head. The crafty old journalist had sent the investigation back to square one, no closer to a resolution. Unless ... he stared at the canisters on the table. Morrison asked Blakeley, "Miles, show Mr. Stein the list of stuff that was in Cook's stomach."

Miles fumbled for the list, dropping his pencil and notebook. As he dug out the folded piece of paper from his breast pocket, Morrison scooped up the items he dropped and exchanged them for the list. He handed it to Stein. Stein unfolded the paper and studied the list. He shook his head. "Odd."

Morrison quizzed him. "Know of anything that might contain those things?"

Stein glanced at the canister, he nodded his head toward it with questioning eyes. Morrison nodded. "Yeah, that's what I'm thinking."

Morrison shifted in his chair. "Anything else we should know about?"

Stein rubbed his chin. "Interesting connection between Elizabeth and Mrs. Nujent."

Morrison ignored the fact that Stein had just admitted to eaves-dropping and was relieved that Blakeley appeared to not notice. Morrison moved on quickly. "Very interesting, but I don't see the connection to Cook."

Stein raised his eyebrows. "Good point."

Blakeley was confused. "What connection?"

Morrison explained, "Nujent and Mrs. Dawson were in the Institute for the Insane at the same time."

Blakeley raised an eyebrow smugly. "Oh, yeah."

He glanced at his partner. "I don't have any more questions, do you Miles?"

Blakeley swelled up, shook his head and leaned back. Morrison stood to shake Mr. Stein's hand. "You will let me know when you guys solve this thing, won't you?"

Stein chuckled and strolled out.

Chapter Fifty-Seven

5:15 P.M. White Feather Hitches a Ride to Canon City

Nᴜᴍʙ ꜰʀᴏᴍ ᴛʜᴇ ɪɴᴛᴇʀᴠɪᴇᴡꜱ, Morrison and Blakeley were silent while walking out to their vehicles. Blakeley's only thoughts seemed to be on his cigarette habit. Morrison was anxious to slide into his SUV and ponder what they learned and try to relax on the drive back to Rockcliffe.

As he pulled the seatbelt across his chest and slipped it into the clip, he felt the bulge of the bottles White Feather had slipped to him and Nujent had provided. He pulled one out of his jacket pocket to look at it again.

Morrison started the engine and reached up to adjust the rear view mirror. When he realized there was a shadowy figure in the back seat, he almost jumped out of his skin. "What?"

Morrison reached for his pistol and spun around to find White Feather asleep in the back seat.

"White Feather!" Morrison exclaimed.

White Feather opened his eyes slowly and then blinked and smacked his lips as consciousness returned to him. Morrison reproached him. "What are you doing?"

White Feather rubbed his eyes with his knuckles. "Going to Canon City with you."

Morrison's heart was pounding. "Dang, White Feather, are you trying to get yourself shot?"

Then Morrison asked, "Why are we going to Canon City?"

White Feather explained, "To investigate the canister."

Morrison pulled a canister from his pocket and noticed for the first time that in small print along the bottom of the label were the words, "Made in Canon City by Dr. Zhang Wei, 719-555-1213."

Morrison turned back to White Feather. "I guess we're going to Canon City, Pardner. But you have to ride up here with me; I'm no chauffeur."

Morrison reached for the microphone with one hand and shifted into Drive with the other, "Gabby, Morrison here, finished interviews. Going to Canon City to investigate a new lead in the case."

Dr. Zhang Wei lived in an aging part of Canon City in a modest but well-kept home. A pretty, young girl around twenty answered the door. Her Oriental features suggested to Morrison that she was probably a relative of Dr. Wei. Speaking through the screen, she asked, "Are you the deputy who called?"

Morrison nodded and touched the brim of his cap. "Yes, Miss, we're here to see Dr. Wei."

She unlatched and pushed open the screen. Inside they found an elderly man sitting under a blanket in a recliner. Morrison smiled and approached. "Dr. Wei?"

The elderly Chinese doctor nodded. Morrison introduced himself and his companion. "I am Deputy Sam Morrison. I am the one who called you. This is White Feather."

Dr. Wei and White Feather scowled at each other. Morrison smiled suspecting the two "men of medicine" were sizing each other up.

Morrison handed him the canister and asked, "Do you recognize this?"

Without removing his arms from under the blanket, he nodded and then directed Morrison with his eyes to a bookcase to his left. One shelf was filled with identical canisters. The young girl moved past Morrison and sat on the arm of Dr. Wei's chair. "I am Susan Ling, this is my grandfather. He is not feeling well today. Maybe I can help you?"

Morrison started to hand her the canister but she countered, "Yes, it is Grandfather's best seller."

"Does your grandfather know a Benjamin Cook that moved into St. Jude Methodist Retirement Center up in the Wet Mountain Valley?"

The young girl turned to her grandfather. Dr. Wei answered in a frail, shaky voice, "I know Benjamin."

Morrison smiled and nodded. "Did he purchase this from you?"

Dr. Wei nodded. "Was it recently?"

Dr. Wei nodded and responded with a heavy Mandarin accent, "Two weeks ago. Said he has new girlfriend. Said she very ... demanding."

Susan Ling explained, "It is a potion for ... it is an aphrodisiac."

Morrison nodded. "Yes, thank you. How many canisters did he buy?"

Dr. Wei hesitated. His granddaughter offered, "Want me to look it up, Wai Gong?"

Dr. Wei closed his eyes, raised his hand and declared, "Twelve; one dozen."

Morrison made a note in his notebook and then crossed his arms. "How do you know Mr. Cook?"

Dr. Wei looked at his granddaughter. She translated for him in Mandarin. He responded to her in Mandarin and nodded with his head over his shoulder. Miss Ling's eyes lit up as if she were experiencing an eureka moment. "Mr. and Mrs. Cook lived next door." She pointed behind her. "I used to play in their yard. Mrs. Cook was such a sweet lady; gave me cookies."

Morrison readied his notepad. "Can you tell me what is in the potion?"

Dr. Wei scowled at him and Susan Ling seemed shocked by his question. Morrison back peddled. "I mean no disrespect, Dr. Wei, we would not steal your formula. We just need to corroborate the contents in Mr. Cook's stomach when he died."

Dr. Wei's eyes widened and Miss Ling gasped. "Benjamin die?" the doctor challenged.

Morrison suddenly felt very rude and thoughtless. "I am so sorry, Dr. Wei. I should have mentioned this up front, but I did not realize that you knew him."

Susan Ling put her arm around her grandfather's shoulder and spoke to him in Mandarin. Dr. Wei shook his head contemptuously. His granddaughter continued, but he stuck out his lower lip and folded his arms. Miss Ling turned to Morrison and explained, "Grandfather feels insulted. Perhaps you should come back another time?"

White Feather stepped up to the old doctor's chair, put his hands together as if in prayer and bowed. To everyone's surprise, he began speaking Mandarin to the doctor. Dr. Wei's face showed surprise, then concern, and then appeared to soften. Miss Ling covered her mouth with her hand and listened intently to the old Cherokee wizard. When he finished speaking, he bowed again and the doctor nodded and looked skeptically at Morrison.

White Feather turned to Morrison, winked and then turned back to the doctor. After a short back and forth, Susan Ling stood and approached Morrison. "They would like for us to step outside."

The young girl hooked her arm around Morrison's and guided him outside. As they stood on the front lawn, Miss Ling pointed out the old Cook house and then answered the real question on his mind. "Mr. White Feather and my grandfather have made a connection. White Feather explained to Wai Gong ..." she paused, smiled and translated, "Grandfather," that he, too, is a man of medicine. He described to Grandfather the ingredients that he puts in the Cherokee love potion."

She shaded her eyes from the sun and looked up into Morrison's eyes. "I think Grandfather may share his ingredients with Mr. White Feather."

When White Feather finally came out of Dr. Wei's house, Morrison and Miss Ling were sitting on the small porch lost in their individual thoughts. White Feather bowed to the young girl and went straight to the vehicle. Morrison jumped to his feet and reached out his hand. "Thank you so much, Miss Ling. It was a pleasure meeting you."

Miss Ling smiled graciously, shook his hand, then returned to the house.

Morrison jumped into the vehicle and immediately turned to White Feather to quiz him, but White Feather interrupted motioning for him to get going. "Do not hesitate. Dr. Wei will be suspicious."

As they pulled away from the Wei house, White Feather folded his arms, closed his eyes and proclaimed proudly, "Case solved."

Chapter Fifty-Eight

8:30 P.M. Stacie Reveals Her Discovery

STACIE FOUND FRANK ROBERTS sitting in the third floor parlor reading. "There you are," she exclaimed.

Frank looked up from his book. When he saw Stacie's twinkling eyes, he smiled at her and put down the book. "Good evening. How was school today?"

Stacie blew through her lips. "Phew, too much homework."

Stacie had such a sincere and bubbling personality, she inspired Frank to want to do something for her. "Can I help you with it?"

Cocking her head to one side, she gave him a most sincere look. "That is so sweet. Know anything about gerontology?"

Frank thought for a moment. "I think I are one."

She burst out laughing, "Good point!"

The happy aide sat down in the chair next to Frank, clasped her hands and placed them on the arm rest facing her aging friend. "Actually, I wanted to tell you what I found out about what we talked about the other night."

He shifted in his chair. "Oh. Well, I haven't turned in a complaint on Nujent. I'm just ..."

Stacie interrupted, "No! Not that. I meant the 'seeing time' thing."

Frank was only a little relieved. Stacie seemed genuinely excited. "It is called synesthesia. And it comes in many different forms. Some see numbers as colors, and some can taste colors."

Frank smacked his lips. "I see numbers as impossible and I never eat my crayons."

Stacie giggled delightfully, reached into her purse and pulled out a scrap of paper. She read, "Psychologist David Brang is studying a bunch of people with an odd form of synesthesia: These people can literally 'see time.'

"Brang's subjects have time-space synesthesia; because they have extra neural connections between certain regions of the brain, the patients experience time as a spatial construct."

She beamed a triumphant smile as she looked at Frank and declared, "So, there you are! It's real."

Frank was unconvinced. Stacie raced on. "And in the article it told about what these people saw and it was exactly what you described to me."

She held out her arms. "White Feather was right!"

Frank shook his head. He could not help feel a little proud to have a "special condition," but at the same time, it made him feel a little bit like a freak. He put a finger to his lips. "We must not speak of this to White Feather. It might cause his head to swell and bust that hollow deer bone he wears in his hair."

The wannabe gerontologist and the geriatric joined in a warm and happy laugh. They truly liked each other; they enjoyed each other's company; they had bonded. It was what Frank imagined having a granddaughter must be like. For Stacie, it was confirmation that she had chosen the right career path.

Thursday

Chapter Fifty-Nine
6:05 A.M. Time Quake

Frank was fast asleep when he felt the tremor. Suddenly, he felt bony fingers gripping his shoulders, shaking him. "Frank, it's time. We must move fast."

Frank realized that it was White Feather dragging him out of bed and handing him clothes to put on. "What is it? An earthquake?" Frank asked.

As they stumbled into the corridor, White Feather corrected him. "No! It's a time quake."

Frank's legs froze up and he could not move. White Feather turned and glared at Ralph. Ralph seemed to understand White Feather's thoughts and grabbed his other arm. Ralph and White Feather dragged him down the corridor to the elevator. Frank protested, "We shouldn't get in an elevator during an earthquake!"

White Feather and Ralph ignored him and pulled him into the dark box. Frank reasoned that the lights were off because of the quake, but the doors slammed shut and the elevator began its descent. Another tremor rattled the elevator and it dropped suddenly to the ground floor, the doors burst open and catapulted the trio into the corridor.

"Quick! Grab him. Not much time!"

Frank felt his friends seize him and run. He tried again to make his legs work but they felt swollen and dead. The patio doors swung open and he could see the gnarly trees by the pond. Another tremor rocked them and the trees split as a great crevasse opened up between them. White Feather and Ralph hurled him into the crevasse where he began spiraling into darkness, spinning, spinning ... and then stillness, quiet.

Amidst the peace he could hear a whirring. He opened his eyes and saw light glowing outside the thin sheet he had pulled over his head. He was cold and felt the chilling breeze from a fan blowing across the billowing sheet. The situation was remotely familiar.

He heard a door open and peeked out to see the whirring metal fan sitting on the table beside the narrow, wooden bed. A delicate hand switched off the fan. "Wake up, Frankie, it's time to get up."

It was his mother's voice. She was smiling at him with a twinkle in her eye. Her hair was auburn and she looked so young. "Hop up and come eat breakfast. You don't want to be late for your first day at school."

She turned and left the room. Across the bed were white shelves with assorted toys and books. It was his room from when he was just a little boy. The light from the morning sun illuminated the room and outside the large windows he could see the long shadow of the house cast across the old detached garage where his basketball hoop was mounted.

"School?"

They parked beside a string of cars blocked by short posts aligned along the front of a huge, two-story, red brick building. Frank followed his mother into a small stucco building nestled amongst several large cottonwood trees. Inside small desks filled three-quarters of the room. A plump, elderly woman sat behind a desk angled in one corner of the front of the room. She rose and smiled at them extending her hand. "Frank! Wake up!"

The pleasant teacher's face turned angry and started shaking him. "Frank!"

The teacher's face changed as Frank began to wake and blink his eyes. In consciousness, he discovered urgency and concern on Stacie's face. "We have to get out of the building, Frank, help me wake the others!"

The three-dozen residents of St. Jude huddled on the grassy front lawn dressed in pajamas and robes. News of a 3.5 earthquake spread around the huddles in whispers. Frank's house shoes were soaked by the heavy dew in the thick grass. His flimsy pajamas were inadequate against the damp morning air. Sirens were wailing in the distance as Stacie, Birdie, and another older woman tried to calm the drowsy, cranky, frightened residents.

The tires of a white BMW sedan squealed as it raced around the corner to the small parking lot in front of the southeast corner of the facility. Mrs. Barkley, the administrator, jumped out of the car and jogged across the lawn to meet with staff.

Frank was shivering next to his friends Albert, Monty, Ralph and White Feather who had managed to find each other. Albert was playing with the dials on his small, portable radio. Ralph grumbled, "It's just a little tremor. Big deal."

"Four tremors." Albert corrected. He found the local station, but the programmed country music was drowned out by the approaching fire department's emergency unit.

Mrs. Barkley shouted out to the residents, "Please! Can I have your attention?"

The crowd got noisier. They could not hear her over the siren of the large, boxed truck overpowering her high-pitched voice as it swerved into the parking lot. Mrs. Barkley raised her hands to try to quiet the crowd, but they were more interested in the firemen.

Slowly, the siren subsided as the men in fire suits climbed out and gathered around an older man holding a radio to his ear. Mrs. Barkley gave up on the residents, strolled over to the men and waited with her hands stuffed into the front pouch of her sweat suit. Frank was jealous of the men, warm in their heavy suits. The four firemen looked almost disinterested as they stood around the older man conversing with some staticky voice on his portable radio.

A sheriff's deputy's SUV raced around the corner and pulled into the gravelly parking lot, spraying pebbles as he slid to a stop. He finished his conversation on his microphone and then slid out of the vehicle.

The elder fireman clipped his radio onto his collar and conferenced with the deputy and Mrs. Barkley and she nodded as she listened to the two men.

Frank turned to his friend, White Feather. "You'll never believe what I was dreaming when the tremors occurred. I dreamed you dragged me out of bed and told me they were 'Time Quakes.'"

Frank laughed, but White Feather's eyes grew large and he grabbed his friend's arm, "The portal!"

Chapter Sixty
The Portal

W HITE FEATHER GRIPPED FRANK'S arm just above the elbow and tugged. "Hurry! We may be too late!"

Frank hesitated but the old Indian was insistent, pulled him away from the crowd and headed around the north side of the old building. Frank dug in his heels, jerked his arm out of the wild Indian's hand and commanded, "What are you doing? Where are we going?"

White Feather's eyes widened and he responded urgently, "The Portal! It's time!"

Frank didn't budge. "It's time for what?"

"Must hurry. May only have one chance."

The Indian raced off toward the back of the building where the familiar park bench, gnarly trees, and pond waited. Frank glanced back at the crowd on the front lawn. The poor old Indian stumbled and fell down. Frank rushed to help him up. "Come on old fool," he complained as they rushed toward the pond.

The two desperate old men stumbled across the back lawn. Frank helped the gasping old Indian to the bench. As they sat down, the gnarly tree faded, oscillated and flickered. Frank dropped onto the bench, rubbed his eyes and looked at the tree again. Now, the tree looked normal. Frank closed his eyes and looked again. The tree looked stubbornly normal.

Frank called to his friend desperately. "Are we too late? Did we miss it?"

The breathless Indian shook his head. "Don't think so."

Frank was frantic. "What do we do?"

The disheveled, but recovering wizard patted his unhinged friend on the leg. "We wait."

Frank looked at the trees, glanced at the Indian, returned to the trees.

White Feather took a deep breath. He regained his composure. "Concentrate on a re-entry point."

Frank studied White Feather. *Is he serious? Is this for real?*

White Feather was steadfast.

Frank sat back, breathed deeply, closed his eyes and searched his life path for the point where he would most like to restart his failed life. He decided on that point, in his early twenties, when he was in college dating two different girls. Maybe this time around, he could choose the right one. Maybe this time he could finish college. Maybe this time his life would work out.

Stacie stood beside Albert and Monty at the windows of the dining room looking out over the west lawn at the bench in front of the pond. Ralph called out from the table as he chewed scrambled eggs, "What are they doing?"

Albert shook his head. "Just sitting on the bench staring at the juniper."

Monty was worried. "Should I go check on them?"

Albert sighed as he returned to the table, "Our breakfast is getting cold. Maybe we can go down after we eat if they are still out there."

Ralph picked up his orange juice. "Probably scared."

Albert paused and glanced back at the odd couple on the bench. Ralph might be onto something. Maybe they are afraid of another tremor. Maybe they are afraid to return inside the old and crumbling building.

Stacie had noticed that Frank and White Feather had mysteriously disappeared while the deputy, firemen, and Mrs. Barkley were in the building making sure it was safe for the residents to return. After the fireman had declared an "all clear," the emergency units had loaded up to leave, and Mrs. Barkley had led everyone back inside. That was when she had discovered Frank and White Feather sitting on the bench in the back yard by the pond.

Stacie glanced at her watch. She would be late for class. She glanced at Albert and Monty and entertained the idea of sending them out with a tray, but decided to give the odd couple more time. An enthusiastic TJ was going around dropping a typed sheet of paper on each table. Ralph snatched it out of her hand before she could lay it down. Albert and Monty sat down. "What does it say?"

Ralph tossed it on the table. "From the sheriff. Says they've solved the murder. Albert did it."

Monty gasped and stared at Albert with desperate anticipation written on his face, Albert picked up the paper. "It's today's interviews."

Albert looked at the expectant Monty. "You're on the list, Walter."

Monty's shoulders dropped. Albert smiled slyly and added, "We're all on the list. Mrs. Barkley, Nujent, Naomi, Katie Mae, Birdie ... you, too, TJ. Looks like all of the staff. We're all to meet here in the dining room at nine o'clock this morning."

Neither aspiring time traveler had spoken for a long while. Frank estimated they had been waiting for well over an hour. He yearned for the sun to rise above the building to bring warmth; his stomach was requesting nourishment; his lips were chapping and his throat was dry.

"Should I go get us something to eat or drink?"

"Shhh!" The determined old shaman answered.

Frank took a deep breath and slumped down on the bench that had become amazingly hard and uncomfortable. He pulled his pajama collar up over his ears, crossed his arms and closed his eyes. He peeked at the tree, just in case, but it had not changed. That was when he felt a presence behind him.

Ralph challenged, "What are you goobers doing out here?"

White Feather shook his head in disgust. Frank glanced back at the three old men sneering at them. He turned to White Feather and whispered, "I think we missed the portal."

White Feather stood. "Sge."

Chapter Sixty-One
Wrapping Up the Case

The Sleuthkateers were sitting in their usual spot in the dining room. It looked like nearly every resident and every staff member was present. The noisy congregation quieted when the sheriff, two deputies and Mrs. Barkley entered the dining room. Mrs. Barkley addressed them first, "May I have your attention, please. We have all been mourning the loss of our friend Benjamin Cook and worried that we might have a murderer in our midst. Sheriff Bailey has brought news of the case today and I asked him to share the news with everyone since we have all shared in the angst of being a suspect."

She held out her hand and the sheriff walked up to stand beside her. "Thank you, Mrs. Barkley."

The administrator stepped back to stand by the deputies. "As you may know, Benny was undersheriff's uncle-in-law. To avoid any conflict of interest, Deputy Morrison headed up the investigation for Wet Mountain County and Miles Blakeley represented CBI. After a very thorough investigation, I believe we are ready to close the case."

He turned toward Morrison. "Sam, want to take over?"

Deputy Morrison walked up to address the room. "Good morning. I would like to take credit for solving this crime, but actually, the credit goes to one of St. Jude's own. White Feather would you join me, please?"

There was a collective gasp when White Feather rose and shuffled up to stand beside the deputy. Morrison offered, "Would you like to tell everyone what you disclosed to me yesterday?"

White Feather waved away the privilege. Morrison resumed, "Alright, well, this case started out promising to be a very difficult one to solve. Almost everyone was a suspect. You all had motive and opportunity and, originally, we thought access to the poison we suspected Mr. Cook died from. But then, it got even more complicated when we discovered that the rat poison we found on the shelf above the drink tray was not the poison used. Plus, we found that neither the tea nor the food was used to deliver the poison."

Morrison winked at Albert Stein and then shifted to wait for the crowd noise to die down. "It was White Feather ..." He paused to find the table where White Feather's friends were sitting. "... and the Sleuthkateers ..." he waved his hand in their direction, "... that figured out that Benny was using an aphrodisiac that he purchased from a Chinese doctor. This potion contained a high dose of strychnine in addition to many other herbs and mixtures used by the Chinese to stimulate ... well, create a love potion."

The room erupted with laughter, side comments and discussions. Morrison raised his hand to calm them down again. "So, it appears that the murderer was ... Benjamin Cook!"

The room erupted again. When they quieted, Morrison finished, "Evidently, Mr. Cook overdosed in anticipation of a pending hot date he had planned for later that day."

This time the room erupted with laughter except for Katie Mae who slowly slid down in her chair to hide under the table.

Elizabeth Dawson stood and glared first at Morrison and then everyone in their turn around the room. Her eyes were red, her face blanched, her hair radiating out like a Tesla plasma globe. "Fools! Those who mock them will feel their wrath. Beware, fools! You blind fools!"

She straightened up and declared in a slow, confident tone, "Penitence wrapped in sad regalia, buried in its penetralia."

She glared at each person in his turn as if her words were profound and explained everything. But, in fact, everyone was confounded by her words.

Morrison blinked, shook his head and resumed, "I'm at a loss to explain that."

Everyone laughed and Elizabeth stormed out of the room. Morrison shook his head again. "Anyway, case closed."

Chapter Sixty-Two

Judy Checks In

FRANK WATCHED WHITE FEATHER weave through the departing crowd to rejoin his friends at their table. It appeared that the old Indian was a hit with the ladies. His friends were waiting with high-fives and praise. White Feather tried to be humble, while Ralph summed it up. "Sleuthkateers one, Sheriff's office zero."

Albert tried to set the record straight. "You solved it, White Feather, not us."

White Feather persisted, "A warrior gets credit for the battle, but he is carried by his horse."

Ralph showed his appreciation for the Native American philosophy. "Do I look like a horse to you?"

They laughed and joked as they tried to flow out of the dining room with the others. Everyone was chattering loudly and happily. A great burden had been lifted off their shoulders. No more Benny Cook to harass them. No more fear that there was a murderer living amongst them.

Frank Roberts saw her before he heard her calling to him. She was standing near the door to the main reception room and waved him over. He managed to elbow his way to her. "Judy! So, good to see you."

The pretty sponsor smiled brightly, "Good to see you, too, Frank. I hardly recognized you without the beard and ... well, the nice clothes."

Frank blushed. "Thank you again for everything."

He followed her into the reception room and they found a couch near the front window. Judy observed, "I can't get over how good you look. St. Jude must be good for you."

Frank took a deep breath. It was true. "What a week it has been!"

Judy smiled and patted his leg. "You are clearly enjoying yourself? Tell me about it."

"Well, I guess you heard about the poisoning?"

Judy's face switched to concern. "Here at St. Jude?"

Frank felt oddly glad that Judy had not heard. "Yes. Benjamin Cook went into a seizure and died at lunch right after you left Sunday. They determined he had been poisoned by strychnine."

Judy put her hand to her mouth. "Oh, dear!"

"Me and four other old geezers have formed a club. We call ourselves the Sleuthkateers. We actually solved the crime!"

Judy burst out laughing and lifted his spirits further with admiring, dancing eyes. "Sleuthkateers. How clever."

Frank shrugged. "Actually Birdie, the cook, came up with the name."

"Oh, yes, I know Birdie. I just love her. So, who did it, Sherlock?"

Frank laughed. He felt like a little kid bragging to his mother. "Actually, he did it to himself. He overdosed on 'Chinese Viagra.'"

"Chinese Viagra? What is that?"

"He had a hot date with Katie Mae, so he got this love potion from an old Chinaman friend that used to be his neighbor. It had strychnine in it. He must have taken triple the dosage just to be sure he was ... well, you know, ready for her."

Judy gasped and tried not to look shocked. "How did you figure it out?"

Frank could not help jabbering like a happy child telling her the whole story in bold and enthusiastic detail. He told her about the caper to break in to the clinic; the clandestine spying from the library; the crack in the wall that let them listen in on the interviews. He even told her about White Feather's attempt to send him back in time.

In a way, he had gone back in time. Back to a time when he was happy; back to a time when life was good and meaningful; back to being his old self. But it was Judy, not White Feather, that had pushed him through that time portal.

Judy smiled at him in a way his mother would have. He felt silly and awkward. "I'm sorry for chattering on. I feel like a kid again. I haven't felt this good in years, thanks to you."

She smiled in a motherly way and replied, "It's about time."

Chapter Sixty-Three
Loosing Their Marbles

S AMANTHA AND TAMMY WERE probably two plays away from victory. Morrison's and Jerry's last marble had been put back. Morrison studied the board and decided that what they needed most was a joker so they could put back the girls' marble. He drew a card and hesitated before looking at it. In his hand he had a three of diamonds, a seven of clubs, a ten of clubs, an eight of hearts, and a nine of spades. He glanced at his partner and then looked at the drawn card. It was a queen. He played it. At least they could get out.

Samantha counted the holes to the finish, "Seventeen." She announced. She drew a card, placed it in her hand and then played a seven. She looked at her partner hoping Tammy had remembered to save a ten. Jerry quickly drew a card and then played an eight and moved their marble back without counting. Sam glanced at his hand to reassure himself he had the three they needed to win.

Without drawing, Tammy tossed a ten on the discard pile as her mother threw up her hands and shouted, "Yes!"

Tammy beamed and reached across the table for a high five. Jerry threw back his head, raised his fists into the air and shouted, "No!"

Morrison laughed joyfully. For just an instant the world grew quiet and motion was suspended giving him that rare opportunity to gaze at his ex-wife and kids like a shopper gazing at a display in a store window. Samantha's eyes sparkled; Tammy was her naturally ebullient self; Jerry was devastated by the shame of losing to the "girls." Morrison's heart leaped with joy, but sank quickly loaded with sadness. His dedication to a thankless job in Denver had cost him this simple happiness of family.

Samantha offered a consolation. "Who wants hot chocolate and ice cream?"

"Sure!" Jerry blurted out and Sam nodded. Tammy joined her mother and proposed, "I'll get the ice cream."

Jerry was still pouting. "I can't believe it! Did you have the three?"

Morrison smiled. "Yeah."

Jerry swung his fist and spun around, "I knew it! Just one move!"

The detective in Morrison observed, "Isn't it amazing how many games are won by just one move? The last game they beat us by one move."

Jerry failed to see the pattern, "Yeah, but we stomped 'em the first game."

Morrison conceded the point. He glanced around the room awkwardly trying to determine where he would sit. Jerry flopped down in the big La-Z-Boy recliner where he used to sit before the divorce. The last time he had visited, Tammy was sitting on the right side of the couch.

Samantha did not sit during that visit, but he felt certain the glider-rocker would still be her favorite, so he headed for the left side of the couch.

Jerry threw the lever and fell back into a prone position as he automatically reached for the remote control and switched on the television. Morrison almost felt offended by the rude gesture, but knew that Jerry's generation could not function without the television babbling in the background or their video games. Jerry picked an odd control device, pushed a button and instantly a team of super heroes battled super villains on the T.V. screen. It was noisy, violent and distracting.

He heard the kettle whistling in the kitchen and his ears honed in to the lively chatter of mother and daughter merrily preparing the treats. This was what normal life was like; what he had squandered; what he was determined to regain.

Tammy stepped down into the den carrying a tray with four bowls of ice cream, Samantha followed with cups of hot chocolate, two in each hand. After passing out the ice cream, as Morrison had guessed, Tammy plopped down on the right side of the couch and put her cup on the end table so she could begin on the ice cream. Samantha placed her cup on a coaster on the end table between the glider-rocker and the couch. She placed a coaster on Morrison's side of the table for him and then slid into the rocker cupping her bowl of ice cream in both hands. She smiled at her ex-husband. "Another case solved?"

Morrison smiled back. He doubted that she was really interested in the "case." She was just being nice. He felt a bit awkward talking about it since cases had been such a painful point of contention in the past. "Yes. Another case solved."

That caught Tammy's and Jerry's attention, Tammy questioned, "Who did it?"

Morrison rolled his head. "Well, actually, Mr. Cook poisoned himself."

Jerry joined in. "Poisoned himself? Suicide?"

It felt good to have their attention. "Actually, no. He overdosed accidentally on a ... well, a love potion."

Tammy's clever mind countered, "Love potion? He had a girlfriend?"

Morrison explained, "Yeah. They were planning a hot date and he gave himself a couple of extra doses for good measure. He didn't know the active ingredient was strychnine."

Tammy frowned; Samantha shook her head. "So sad."

Jerry was intrigued. "Why would they put strychnine in a love potion?"

Morrison could see from the blank expressions that no one knew anything about strychnine. He offered, "Used to be the main ingredient in rodent poison. But in smaller doses, it was used by athletes like a physical enhancement drug."

Jerry was curious. "What does it do to you when you overdose?"

"Ooo, gross!" Tammy protested.

"Jerry ..." Samantha scorned.

Morrison could not resist. "Witnesses reported that he vomited and then went into convulsions. Some reported that they thought he was being strangled by ghosts."

Jerry's eyes brightened. "Cool."

Tammy's face contorted. "How disgusting."

Samantha whispered, "Oh, Sam, that's enough."

Sam added, "The curious thing is that one of residents had warned him that ghosts were coming after him right before that and that they would strangle him."

It was just too much. Jerry hooted. Tammy slammed her bowl on the end table and Samantha shook her head. "How are we supposed to enjoy our ice cream now?"

Morrison shut up. Jerry grabbed his bowl and started shoveling down the ice cream and Tammy raked her fingers through her hair, while Samantha smiled and tentatively dipped her spoon in the ice cream and took a small bite.

Jerry spoke through his mouthful of ice cream, "They gonna give you a raise or something?"

Morrison grinned, saying, "Probably not. I didn't actually solve this case—White Feather did."

Samantha's eyes twinkled. "Oh, that nice Native American that helped you with David's case?"

Tammy remarked, "Maybe you should deputize him."

Morrison shrugged. "Yeah, maybe so."

After thinking about it for a moment, Morrison jinxed the valley by saying, "Nah, this place doesn't have enough cases for another homicide detective."

Morrison glanced around the room. "Truthfully, there's not enough for one full-time homicide detective. Maybe now I'll have more time for stuff like marbles."

Samantha smiled. "It's about time."

Sneak Peek:

Ghosts of St. Jude

Book 3
A White Feather Mystery

by Courtney Miller

Excerpt

THE BULKY METAL BOX was getting heavier with each step. Frank's shoulders were aching from the load. He followed Ralph through the bushes and trees to the west side of the St. Jude property.

One last push through the brush put them in a large clearing. A six-foot stone fence defined the western border of St. Jude. An old and rotting wooden door set ajar inside a three-and-one-half foot gap in the fence. About fifteen feet from the gate, an old cistern made of the same stones sat crumbling. What was once the roof lay broken and rotting to one side. Dry, warped planks lay across the rounded top to cover the abandoned well.

"Set it down there," Ralph demanded pointing to a spot in the center of the clearing.

Albert, Monty, and White Feather crowded around to watch the grumpy ex-construction engineer unroll two wires wrapped around a simple control box roughly the size of a sandwich. He plunged the firing caps into the soft dough-like substance he had used to line the rim of the lid of the can.

"What is that, Silly Putty?" Frank asked.

C4, was the simple answer.

Frank's face grew red. "I've been carrying a box lined with plastic explosives?"

Ralph was walking away stringing the wire behind him. "It's harmless without the blasting caps."

His four friends scurried away from the box.

Albert challenged his cantankerous colleague. "What are you planning here, Rudolph?"

Ralph had reached the end of the twenty-foot wires and was standing facing the metal box holding the control box. "I'm going to blow the lid off the damn thing like we talked about."

His friends gasped. Frank stated the obvious. "You'll blow us all up."

Ralph was contemptuous. "You don't know anything about C4, do you?"

Frank snapped back, "Do you?"

Ralph shrugged. "Trained on it in the military."

Frank, familiar with military training, was not satisfied. "Ever actually use it?"

White Feather cautiously herded his friends around behind the old stone cistern. Monty was concerned for his friend. "Better get behind something, Ralph."

Ralph huffed. "Not a problem. C4 will direct the explosion toward the surface of the box. I'm perfectly safe."

With that, he flipped the switch on the control box. KABOOM!

The four men hit the ground behind the cistern. Although expecting a loud explosion, they were not expecting to feel the concussion of the blast from C4. It left their ears ringing loudly.

When Frank peeked over the top of the cistern amid the concentrically unfurling smoke, he saw that the box had vanished. "You blew it up, you idiot!"

Ralph's shirt and short pants were shredded, revealing his undershirt and shorts. His body was smoking and his hair singed. They ran up to him and discovered that the front of his body was black with soot. "Ralph! Are you alright."

The smoldering, crooked old man coughed black smoke out of this mouth. White Feather proclaimed, "Here it comes."

He was staring into the sky. The others looked up to watch the smoking, metal can hurtling toward the ground. The sleuthkateers naturally ducked before realizing that the can was falling outside the rock fence.

They followed White Feather to the gate. He pushed on the dilapidated gate and instead of swinging open, the old door fell flat. The Sleuthkateers rushed through and scrambled west toward where the box had dropped. Frank was in the lead when he stopped abruptly and threw out his hand, palm facing his friends. He had stumbled upon the edge of a deep ravine about twenty feet deep and seventy-five feet across.

His friends rushed up and stared curiously into the ravine except for White Feather who pointed across the ravine at a tall fence wearing a crown of curling razor wire. Inside the compound Albert recognized the significance of the long, rounded green houses and a dozen or more large water tanks, and simply stated, "A grow site."

Walter was confused. "Grow what?"

Ralph trudged up and declared, "Wacky weed."

Frank asked, "Marijuana?"

White Feather put his hands on Frank's and Albert's shoulders and whispered urgently, "Get down."

Six rough-looking men in camouflaged fatigues were standing in the center of the compound surrounding the crater where the box had impacted. They were pulling assault rifles off their shoulders and one was shouting and pointing at the old men.

White Feather, the only one who had faced an enemy on the battlefield, gave the command. "Run!"

The wobbly old men gave their best imitation of running as they scurried back to the safety of the stone wall. White Feather stood watch at the gate while his friends lay gasping on the ground behind the stone barrier.

Albert was the first to try to size up their situation. "Must be an illegal grow site. We must call the sheriff."

White Feather replied firmly, "We must not speak of this again."

Albert was confounded. "What? What do you mean, White Feather? We have to report it to the authorities."

White Feather kept his eyes trained to the west. "How will you explain the box?"

Ralph got it. "And the illegal C4."

White Feather pulled an old gourd rattle out of his belt and started bouncing slightly, shaking the rattle and chanting. The others did not understand Cherokee, but clearly understood the significance of his prayer.

About the Author

Courtney Miller is the multi-award winning author of the seven-book series, *The Cherokee Chronicles*. He is considered an expert on ancient Native American culture and incorporates that knowledge into his writing. He has written over 200 articles on the art, archeology, astronomy, culture and history of ancient Native America for Native American Antiquity and other online ezines.

His seven-book series, *The Cherokee Chronicles,* has received multiple awards and widespread praise from the Cherokee community for its authenticity. In his new series, The White Feather Mysteries, Miller once again shows his award-winning talents bringing to life fresh characters with a twisting plot and surprise ending.

Courtney now lives in the Wet Mountain Valley of Colorado with his wife, Lin. He enjoys playing golf and also is active in the local Rotary club.

www.ingramcontent.com/pod-product-compliance
Lightning Source LLC
Chambersburg PA
CBHW020931120726
47905CB00008B/2474